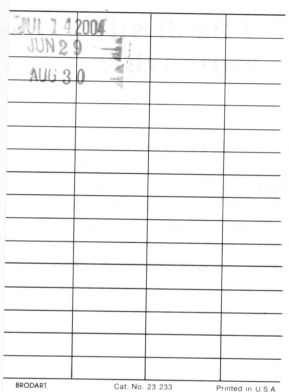

Also by Helen Armstrong

The Road to Somewhere
The Road to the River

The Road to Adventure

Helen Armstrong

Illustrated by Steve Dell

Dolphin Paperbacks

First published in Great Britain in 2003
by Dolphin paperbacks
a division of the Orion Publishing Group Ltd
Orion House
5 Upper St Martin's Lane
London WC2H 9EA

A catalogue record for this book is available
from the British Library

Printed in Great Britain by
Clays, St Ives plc

ISBN 1 84255 227 9

To Clare –
'For we like sheep'

The Road to Adventure

CHAPTER 1

I am round and brown and bright as all your buttons. I am Ratty and I live at the City Farm. Today I am not quite so bright because I am wet.

It is raining. I sit in the doorway of Cow's shed and look out. I am cold and I am wet. The rain blows in upon my brown ratty face. There are raindrops on my whiskers. They drip off onto the ground on each side of my long nose. I am not happy. Not by a long wet straw.

Cow stands next to me. Cow is my friend. She is munching her feed and swinging her tail and smiling. The rain outside does not bother her.

Woolly Woolly Baa Lamb is huddled with his sheep friends in one corner of the shed. Woolly is a fierce and fighting lamb. He likes to be out and doing. Sitting in a corner does not suit him but the rain is too much for him. So he sits there and chews his feed and frowns all over his curly face.

I peer out and I stare this way and that. Perhaps something will happen. Then I see a car pull up at the farm gate. The door swings open and out jumps a yellow dog.

I am up on my four feet in a second. I know who this is! Chee! Chee is a doggo that I met on my last adventure. She is small and yellow and wild as can be. She is a good friend for a wet day, or any day come to that.

'Chee is here!' I call out to Cow and Woolly. 'Now we will have some fun!'

Cow blinks her eyes and nods her head. Woolly grumbles in his corner. 'No fun today,' says he. 'Wet is no fun at all.' He frowns and screws up his hard little mouth.

'I am glad Chee has come,' says Cow. 'Chee is a good and cheerful friend. She cannot help being a doggo after all.' Cow does not like doggos but she does like Chee.

Chee is jumping and skipping down the wet path towards us. Her person is talking to Hat Man. Perhaps Chee will spend the afternoon with us. Her person goes to work some days and on those days Hat Man looks after Chee.

'Friends, oh friends!' sings out Chee. She is skipping between the puddles on her curved yellow legs. 'I have news for you I have! Oh I have I have!'

She leaps over the last patch of water and here she is in the cowshed. Chee is bigger than me, of course she is. But she is the smallest doggo you ever did see. Small, and yellow, and quick, and cleverer than you would believe. She has a round head and round eyes and a curly tail and she talks high and squeaky and loud enough for all the farm to hear her.

'Oh ho!' says Chee. 'You look a sad bunch today. But not for long! Hear my news!' She begins to dance upon her yellow legs and wag her tail. She throws her head back. 'I'm a star! I'm a star! I'm a star!' sings Chee.

I stare and so does Cow. What does Chee mean?

Woolly Woolly Baa Lamb does not stare. He glares at her with his hard blue eyes and flaps his ears. 'A star is something bright in the sky. You are little and yellow and on the ground,' says he. 'You are not a star nor nothing like it. And perhaps you could stop shouting. Some of us want to snooze here.'

'You are a crosspatch Woolly,' says Chee. 'I will tell you what I mean if you will listen.'

So Woolly flaps his ears again and looks at her and says nothing at all. That is enough for Chee. 'I am a star,' says Chee. 'A television star. A famous doggo. A Personality. That's me.' She wags her tail and dances on her four yellow feet.

'What are you talking about?' says I.

Chee blinks her round eyes and sits down on a patch of straw. She has a story to tell. She must be comfortable.

'Well,' says she, 'I went to the vet. Had to – I had a poorly eye and they put drops in it. Humph!' says Chee. 'I did not like that.'

I have never been to the vet. It does not sound so nice I must say but Hat Man says it is important. He even says he will take me if I get poorly, but ratties are never poorly I am glad to say.

'Are you listening, Ratty?' says Chee. I nod my head and on she goes. 'When I was there, and my person too of course, we saw people with cameras for the television. They said it was for a programme about pets and vets.'

We nod our heads. We have seen television once, or twice maybe.

'Anyway,' says Chee, 'the Chief Man saw me and said he wanted me on the programme. He said people would like me! I am the greatest!' sings Chee. 'So that is my news. I will be on the television and you can all see me and that will be the best ever.' Her tail is wagging so fast it is just a yellow blur.

'Humph!' says Woolly. 'That is not so exciting.'

Chee looks at him crossly for a moment. Then she shakes her head and stamps a paw upon the ground. 'I forgot the most important bit!' she says. 'Of course it is exciting that I am on the television but there was something more.' Her face is not so happy now. Her ears droop. Her tail stops wagging.

'Listen harder, Woolly,' says she. 'There was a pup at the vet's too. The hospital people said he was lost. But he was not lost. He ran away. He had been treated not right you know. So he ran away and someone found him. That is how he got to the Animal Hospital,' says she.

'Mmmm' says Woolly. He looks interested now.

'The pup told me that he had lived with lots of other puppies in a cold dark place out in the country, a barn he said. In a place with lots of sheep. Two bad men looked after them. Then the men put him in the back of a van and brought him to the city. And he ran away! He will be fine now but all those poor puppies! It is not right!'

Woolly is half sitting up now. 'Lots of sheep,' says he. His eyes are gleaming. 'And in the country too. Ratty, Ratty, perhaps I could help the puppies.'

'What do you mean?' says I.

'Well, you see,' says Woolly, 'If the pups are in the country and there are lots of sheep, I could go there and I would not be noticed. I can help the pups! I know I can.'

Woolly may be right. He cannot go out of the farm most times because people notice sheep in a town. But a sheep place in the country? Perhaps he could go there.

I look at him with my beady ratty eyes. 'Maybe you could,' says I.

Chee's eyes sparkle. 'Oh yes!' says she. 'Oh yes. You could! Woolly and Ratty too. How exciting! I'm sure you could!'

I would like an adventure. And Woolly would like one too I can see. My whiskers shake with excitement. This could be fun.

All this time Cow is standing munching. She has a funny look upon her face. 'What about me?' says Cow through a mouthful of hay.

'What do you mean?' asks Chee. She wrinkles her yellow forehead.

'I do not want to miss an adventure,' says Cow.

'It is not an adventure yet,' says Chee.

'But it will be,' says Cow. 'I can see that.'

Cow's face is a kind and smiling sort of face. And cheerful. But not now. Her face is lumpy and sad-looking. Her tail is twitching.

'But Cow, you are so big. Bigger than me,' says Woolly. 'And the pup did not say anything about cows, you know.'

Cow looks down glumly at her feet. 'I am sorry, friends,' says she, 'I am a selfish sort of cow, I think. I like to have adventures! I do not want to be left behind!' She almost moos at this.

Hat Man sticks his head around the cowshed door. He is the man in charge of the City Farm. He is a kind man. 'Are you all right Cow?' says he. 'That was a funny noise there.'

Cow nods her head. It is a sad nod. Hat Man looks

puzzled but he shrugs his shoulders and off he goes.

Chee is looking worried too and it takes a lot to worry Chee. 'This is not good,' says Chee. 'You are a hero cow, we know that. But you are so big you know. How can you get out of the farm? How can you have adventures?'

A tear runs down Cow's face. 'I am in prison,' says Cow. 'I cannot get out. It is a nice prison I know. But I am not a prison sort of cow.'

'Oh Cow,' I cry. I look at her sad sad face. I remember our first great adventure when she ran from Farmer's farm. 'We will think of something. We will.'

We all stare at Cow. What can we do?

Then Cow lifts her big head. Her eyes begin to gleam. Cow's eyes are soft and dark. I have not seen them gleam like this. She straightens her lumpy cow back. She flaps her big ears until they look like heavy wings on each side of her head. She wriggles and shakes herself from her nose to her tail end.

Then she looks at us.

'Do not worry, friends,' says she in quite a different sort of voice. 'You do not have to think of anything. Leave it to me. I am a big cow now. I will find a way.'

'Oh Cow,' says I. 'Be careful.'

But it is too late for that. Cow is not a careful sort of cow. Careful cows like to live in prison places. They stay happy in one place and munch and doze and munch again and are as milky as can be. Not Cow.

Cow is munching her food again now. She looks peaceful but she is not. I know that.

'Well, Cow, if you are sure,' says Chee.

Cow nods her head and munches on. I stare at her and try to see what she is thinking.

'Come on, Ratty,' says Chee. 'Let us think about saving these pups.'

Woolly lurches up onto his four hooves. 'The rain has stopped,' says he. 'Let us go out and eat some grass and make a plan.' Woolly is right. The rain has stopped. The sun is shining now and all the puddles gleam with brightness.

'Come on Ratty,' says he. Out he trots into the paddock. Chee trots after him. I look at Cow one more time but she pretends she does not notice me and eats her hay.

So out I go.

Chee has found a bale of straw to sit on. Woolly

stands on his four feet and pulls at the wet green grass with his sharp straight teeth. I perch upon a bucket that is upside down.

Woolly lifts his head. The grass sticks out of his mouth like a green fringe. 'I can eat and listen too,' says Woolly. 'Please tell us what the pup said, Chee.'

Chee begins. 'This pup tells such a sad story,' says she. 'He lived in the dark and the cold. They were all in a barn and there were lots of sheep in the fields.'

'Lots of sheep sounds good,' says Woolly through his grassy mouthful.

'But where are the pups' mothers?' I ask. 'They must have mothers you know.'

'The bad men took their mothers away,' says Chee.

'That is so sad,' says I. 'We must help if we can. But how can we find them?'

'You will have to talk to Pup,' says Chee.

'Easy said,' says I, 'but not so easy done. How can I speak to him when he is at the Animal Hospital?'

'It is not easy,' says Chee. 'And he goes to his new home tomorrow. He told me. You must talk to him today.'

I bristle my long whiskers. 'Chee,' says I, 'hospitals do not like ratties. No they do not. I cannot go to the hospital and say – where is that pup? I would not last long that way I think.'

Chee puts her yellow head on one side and stares at me with her round round eyes. 'Ratty, friend Ratty,' says she, 'I have a plan.'

I shake at that. Chee's plans are too exciting for a ratty who likes a safe and happy life. 'Tell me,' says I.

'I will get you into the hospital!' says Chee. She turns to Woolly who is jumping just a bit upon his four hard hooves. He is wide awake now.

'Woolly,' says she, 'you must stay here for now. Ratty and I will go to find out more. Then you can start your adventure!' She skips up onto her four yellow feet. 'Come on Ratty,' says she, 'stick close to me and we will find the pup. You'll see!'

She waves her tail at Woolly and at Cow. Cow is peering out of the cowshed door. The sun shines warm upon her patterned forehead. She is smiling in a gleamy sort of way.

'Come on Ratty!' yelps Chee. Off she goes running

and skipping up the farm path towards where Hat Man is mending a fence.

Then all at once 'Yip!' goes she. 'Yip!' and 'Yip!' again. It is a strange sort of noise. A soft and breathy sort of noise. But loud too. Hat Man looks up. 'What is that?' says he. He stops. He turns to look.

'Ooooooh,' wails Chee.

She topples over onto her side. Thud! She hits the path. She lies still as a stone.

Hat Man gasps and throws his arms into the air. 'Oh goodness me,' says Hat Man. 'Poor Chee. She has collapsed. We must get her to the hospital quick as quick.'

And then I understand.

CHAPTER 2

I understand at last. This is Chee's plan. This is how we are to get into the Animal Hospital.

Hat Man comes running down the path. He leans over Chee. 'Oh Chee,' says he, 'your person trusted you to me and now this happens. You are a poor sick doggo. We must get you to the vet straight away.'

He rushes over to his van and opens the doors. Then he goes back and picks up Chee. He carries her to the van. He lays her carefully on the van floor. He has forgotten about me. In I leap and hide behind the wheel arch. He closes the van doors.

As the van starts up, Chee opens one bright eye and whispers to me. 'Pup is in the cages at the back of the hospital, Ratty. You will have to follow me.'

The van stops. Out leaps Hat Man. He opens the van doors and reaches in for Chee. I slide past him when his back is turned and jump down under the van. He strides off and I dodge after him. I scurry and creep and follow until he reaches the doors of the Animal Hospital.

Hat Man steps forward to the big doors with Chee in his arms. A lady holds the door open for him. Her long coat blows in the wind. It hides me from people eyes.

'Thank you,' says Hat Man stepping through. I slide after him, quick and quiet.

We are in a square room with chairs along two sides. On the far side is a high counter. Hat Man goes to the counter. I jump sideways and hide under a chair. I huddle there and wait. There is someone sitting on the chair above my head. They do not know that I am there.

There is a doggo opposite me. A big doggo. He sees me. He can hardly believe his doggo eyes. He stares. Then he opens his wide doggo mouth. He flashes his white doggo teeth.

'Rat!' he roars. He jumps to his feet. He leaps across the room to get to me. His lead comes tight around his person's hand. Up she pops like a rabbit. Up and forward across the room.

'Aaah,' she goes. She almost falls on her face upon the floor. Just in time she stops and heaves back upon the lead. The doggo's white teeth flash in front of me. His breath stings hot upon my trembling nose.

'What are you doing?' yells his person. 'Stop that! Stop that at once. Bad dog!'

'Rat! Rat! Rat!' howls the doggo.

The person on my seat is shaking so hard I can hear the chair legs rattle. 'How fierce he is!' says a squeaky voice above my head. 'Will he eat me? Or my cat here?'

'No! no!' says doggo's person. She is very cross now. She is red in the face. 'I do not know what is the matter with him. He is a good dog most times. I will take him out. We will wait outside.'

Doggo's eyes glare at me. But he can do nothing. Out he goes on his lead to wait in the cold. 'Bad dog,' says his person as they step out through the swing doors.

Hat Man is talking to the girl at the counter. 'Take poor Chee straight through,' says the girl. 'Through here,' she says and opens a door behind her.

This is my chance. I skim under the line of chairs. Behind people feet, past cat boxes, past paws and coats and bags. I reach the end of the line of chairs. There is

14

no time to think. Out I slide and through the door just as it swings closed again.

I hear a voice behind me in the waiting room. 'What was that?' it says. 'Did I see something there?'

But no one replies. I am through. I am safe for now. Where next?

I am in a narrow passageway. Ahead Hat Man walks with Chee in his arms. I must hide! There is a cupboard in the passage. The door is just ajar. In two leaps I am inside it. I must wait now. Wait and see what happens.

It is a long wait. Waiting is boring so I curl up and snooze. A rat snooze. That means I close my eyes and dream the time away, but all the while my round ears twitch this way and that. They listen out for trouble.

A good thing too. I snap awake in a moment. My ears hear feet along the passageway. Feet and voices.

'Goodnight,' calls someone from the passage outside my door. I crouch down even tighter into the dark. The door pulls open. Snap. Whoosh. A person takes a coat down from a hanger above my head.

'Night!' calls another voice further away. Then silence.

Time to go. I edge to the cupboard door. I peer out. I am as careful as can be. Perhaps someone is left behind. But no. I look. I sniff the air. I listen. No one.

The light is still on but not so bright as before. At the end of the passage I hear noises. Snuffles, yelps, purring, and a snore.

Then I hear Chee. 'Ratty! Now! Come quick! Quick as you can!'

Up I leap and off I go. Out of my cupboard, along the passage and with one big bound into a high bright room.

I stop and I gasp.

Cages. It is a room of cages! There are cages along each wall. They stretch from down here by the floor almost to the ceiling.

And here is Chee. Bright as a button inside her cage and looking out for me.

'Ratty! You must hurry. Talk to Pup quick as quick and then get away. And Oh Ratty' she cries. 'It almost

went all wrong! My person came. She wanted to take me home! I had to lie so still. I had to look so poorly. The vets don't know what is the matter with me. Of course they don't! They are keeping me here until tomorrow. Then I can be better.'

She smiles her wild smile. Then she points her yellow nose to a cage at the far end of the row. 'That's him,' says she. 'That's Pup. Go and talk to him. Hear what he has to say.'

I trot over towards Pup's cage. He is curled up in a ball. His eyes are shut. His round paws cover his black and shining nose. His skin is smooth and black and soft like velvet.

He is asleep.

'Wake up!' I squeak. 'Wake up! I have to talk to you.'

His ears wobble for a moment. Then they fall flat again. He breathes a soft sigh.

'Wake up!' I screech, loud as I can, close to his ear. 'Wake up!'

He is up in a moment. He staggers on his puppy legs. He turns and stares at me. 'A ratty!' says he. 'You must be a ratty. I have never met a ratty before.' He stares at me in a round-eyed friendly sort of way.

'Yes, I am Ratty,' says I. 'Chee has told me about your puppy friends. She says you all lived in a barn with bad people looking after you. I and my friends can help. Perhaps we can rescue your friends. But first we need to know how we can find them.'

He is a clever pup I will say. Now that he is awake he

sees it all in a moment. 'She told you, did she?' says he looking across at Chee. He wags his tail in thanks. 'You are just in time. I am going to a new home. Lots of people saw me on the television. They all want me to live with them.' He looks very pleased at this. 'So now I have a home of my own.'

He smiles so wide that I can see all his white puppy teeth. I smile back at him. But there's work to do.

'How can we find your friends?' I ask. 'How can I find the barn you told Chee about? Where is it?'

He frowns and leans his head to one side. 'It is a high dark barn,' says he, 'and cold.' He thinks again. 'There were lots of sheep,' says he. 'We heard them outside and sometimes they came into the barn. All the sheep have blue circles on their backs.'

'Mmm,' says I. 'It is not so easy to find sheep with blue circles. Is there anything else?'

'It is not so far from here,' says he. 'The van drove in quite quick. And there are trains close by. That's what the sheep said they were. Loud noisy things. What is a train?' he asks. He looks at me with his round black eyes and wrinkles his soft forehead.

But I am not listening to him now. My ears have heard another kind of noise. A quiet noise, the noise a person makes when no one is meant to hear. A whisper. And a scraping scratching sound.

It comes from the door to the outside. I stare. The handle of the door moves down. Slowly and gently. Then someone pushes against the door. I hear his shoulder on the wood. Once. Then again. Stronger this time.

'It's locked,' says a high squeaky sort of voice.

'Bound to be!' says another. It is not squeaky at all. It is low and gruff and fierce-sounding.

The black pup has frozen to a statue. His ears stand up. His eyes stare wide. The dark hair ripples on his soft puppy back. 'I know them!' he whispers. 'That's Tone! That's Jeth.'

'You know them! Who are they?' I hiss. All the time I keep my sharp eyes upon that door and on that handle.

'They have come for me!' says Pup. He is whimpering now. He squirms and looks about him. 'They will take me away. They will. They will.'

'Hear that?' says the squeaky voice behind the door. 'Listen to that yowling. That's him.'

'You're right there, Tone,' says the gruff voice. It must be Jeth. 'Whinging little pest he always was. But we're owed good money for him. I'm not going to lose it now.'

'The television said he was heading for a new home,' says Tone.

'He doesn't need a new home,' says Jeth. 'No indeed.' He laughs and it is not a nice kind of laugh. 'We've found a nice home for him we have. Well perhaps not so nice, but they'll pay money for him. So let's get on with it.'

They push against the door. Once and again. The

door groans but does not move.

'Stand to one side,' says Jeth. 'I'll give it a go with this.' There is a grating sound of metal. The door bends just a little.

Chee presses her face to the wire of her cage. She whispers down to me. 'Ratty! Ratty! They will get in soon. That door is bending more than I like. Pup will be lost and all his friends too. Set off the alarm!'

'What do you mean?' I squeak.

'Up there,' she calls out. 'Look!'

I look up. High on the wall above the cages is a tiny box. An alarm? How can that be an alarm?

'Block the beam!' howls Chee. 'That hole – see it?' She is right. There is a tiny hole in the side of the box. 'Get in front of it! Wave your tail at it! Do something! Set it off!'

I turn to Pup. He is staring at the door. His body shakes. His breath comes fast and light as if he had been running many a mile. But he has run nowhere. There is nowhere to run. He is trapped and these men have come for him.

The door bulges again. They have almost smashed it.

I must do something. I begin to climb up to the alarm box, up the wire fronts of the cages. I pull with my short front legs. I scrabble and push with my back legs. It is hard work for a fat ratty. My paws scratch on the wire mesh. My shoulders ache. But up I go. Up and up.

One more heave and I am there. In the gap along the high cage tops.

Three long leaps and I am by the alarm box.

'Block the beam!' shouts Chee.

I stare at the box. I step in front of it. I grab it with my two front paws. I bend my head down low and stare into that little hole on the side.

Bee-Bah! Bee-Bah! Bee-Bah!

A great noise fills the room. Bee Bah! It clangs against the walls and windows. It hurts the creatures' ears. They stick their paws over their heads and cower in the corners of their cages.

Then Crack! Thump! Crash! The door smashes open.

In tumble two men. One is big with a square hard face. The other is little and skinny.

'What is that noise, Jeth?' says the skinny one. He has little pale eyes. His mouth has fallen open. He is staring this way and that.

'You are an idiot, Tone!' yells Jeth, the big one. 'That is an alarm! That's what that is!'

'Where is that pup? Where is he?' asks Tone.

'Well, we know he's here. But we've not got long to find him. Not now,' growls Jeth. He looks over his shoulder. He is worried.

'I'll check all the cages, that's what I will do,' says Tone.

Then in the distance I hear another Bee-Bah noise. Far away but coming closer.

Bee-Bah Bee-Bah shouts the alarm above my head. 'This way, this way,' it calls.

Bee-Bah calls back the noise outside in the dark night.

'Police!' shouts Jeth. He shouts so loud that the cages shake. 'We're off! I'm not getting done for one pup. We could lose everything. Come on you!' he yells at Tone. He grabs Tone's arm and pulls him towards the door.

'But I've found him!' squeaks Tone. He has seen Pup hiding in his cage.

'Too late!' roars Jeth. 'They're almost here. Out!'

He pulls and pushes Tone out of the door. I hear their feet pounding off into the darkness.

I hear the Bee-Bah coming closer and closer.

From my high perch, I look at Pup. He is standing at the front of his cage. He is staring at the open door. He starts to smile. I see his white teeth flash. He is happy. I am pleased that he is happy but it is too late to talk to him now.

'Run! Run, Ratty!' calls Chee. 'You must go now Ratty to save your skin. Go or it will be the end for you.'

'You're right,' say I.

I leap along the cage tops. I grab the corner post. I slide down from top to bottom. My paws hurt but I do not care. I am not stopping now.

Thud! I reach the hard floor. Across the floor I leap in one long bound. Out through the door I go. Into the dark. Into the shadows. Just as two policemen come running round the end of the building.

They do not see me. They are not looking for me.

They run past and disappear through the bright square of the doorway.

I wait for a moment. Then I turn and scamper off towards my own bed. I have a lot to think about.

CHAPTER 3

I lie in my warm rat bed and I sleep and I think a bit. But mostly I sleep. Suddenly I leap up because Woolly Woolly Baa Lamb is bleating at me very loud indeed.

'Tell me! Tell me!' bleats Woolly Woolly Baa Lamb. He is jumping up and down on his four legs. 'Tell me what Pup said! Tell me how we start on our adventure!'

I sit back and blink at him. 'I am just woke up,' says I crossly. 'I must have my breakfast before I say another word.'

Woolly knows about eating. He stands there while I go and look for one of Pig's apples. He tries to be patient while I pull the apple back across the yard. He watches me while I take hold of it with my two front paws.

I open my mouth very wide and take a big bite. The apple juice runs down my whiskers. It is very good indeed. Woolly stamps his foot. 'Try to eat fast Ratty,' he says. 'I do so want to know.'

Just then there is a car noise in the road outside the farm. The car stops. We hear the car door open. Out comes Chee's person smiling all over her face. And Chee jumps out after her, smiling just like her person.

Hat Man comes hurrying up. 'You've got her back!' says he.

'Yes yes,' says Chee's person. 'Chee is out of the hospital. She is well as can be! They do not know what was the matter yesterday but she is good as new now!'

'I am glad to hear it,' says Hat Man. 'I was so worried, you know.' Then off they go for a drink of tea and a chat.

Chee comes leaping and skipping down the path wagging her tail and grinning all over her yellow face. 'I am out at last!' she calls to us. 'And Pup has gone to his new home. Now we have things to think about.'

I haven't finished my apple so Chee goes off to talk to Cow. Woolly munches grass and stares about him. I wash my whiskers and my paws and then I am ready.

'Cow! Chee!' I call out. 'Would you like to talk plans now?'

Woolly frowns. 'It is not their adventure,' says Woolly. 'It should just be you and me, Ratty friend.'

'That may be so,' says I, 'but they are good and clever friends, Woolly lambkin, and we will see what we will see.'

Out come Cow and Chee from the cowshed. The

sun is shining down upon the corner of the green paddock. That is where we go. Cow lies down, slow as slow like ever was. Woolly stands and twitches his tail. Chee sits on the warm grass and I sit on my bucket.

'Shall I tell them, Ratty?' says Chee.

'Yes please,' says I. So Chee tells Woolly and Cow about last night and Jeth and Tone and the policemen and what Pup said.

Cow snorts. 'Those men do not sound nice men to me,' says she. 'I am glad that Pup is safe now.'

Woolly shakes his curly head. He looks puzzled. 'I do not know how we can find these other pups,' says he. 'There must be lots of barns, you know.'

'Yes yes,' says Chee. 'But not so many near the trains, and near the city too you know. And only one with blue ring-sheep. I do not think it will be so hard to find once you begin,' says Chee.

Woolly's eyes go bright. 'Trains?' says he. 'I had forgot about the trains.' He glances over his woolly shoulder. Just beyond the City Farm, there is a high steep bank. It stretches from here to far away. On the top of the bank is the railway line. We see trains every day. And hear them too. 'Trains,' says he again.

'You see,' says Chee, 'you can follow the railway line! All the way into the country!'

Woolly begins to dance on his hard hooves. His eyes glow. His tail whisks to and fro. 'You are right! You are right! You are right!' he bleats.

'You look a dangerous lambkin,' says I. 'You look so dangerous that Hat Man will notice. You had better calm down.'

'I am a dangerous lambkin,' says Woolly, 'and no bad men can stop me!'

I look at Chee. 'Will you come with us, Chee?' says I. 'You like adventure, that I know.'

Chee shakes her head. 'I cannot come,' says she. 'I have worried my person so much with being poorly. She will cry if I run off again. I must stay and be a good doggo. I will stay here with Cow,' says she.

Then she turns her round eyes to Cow. Cow looks back at her. Then Cow winks!

I stare. I gasp. I have known Cow a long and long time. I have seen her eyes blink and stare and close and even cry. But never in that long time have I seen Cow wink. What does it mean?

But she has stopped winking now. She is looking up at the sky in a peaceful sort of way. She hums a little tune so quiet I can hardly hear it.

'Mmm,' says I. 'Then it is just you and I, Woolly my friend. When should we go?'

'I think tomorrow will be best,' says Woolly. 'First thing in the morning you know. As soon as Hat Man opens the door of my shed.'

I nod my ratty head. 'That sounds fine to me,' says I. 'Tomorrow it will be.'

So that is that. The plan is made.

The sun shines on. We chat. We snooze. Then visitors

come. It is a quiet sort of day. I am glad of that. Tomorrow will be too exciting by half. That is what I think.

When the dark comes, Woolly is shut in the sheep house with his friends. There is no way out at night.

Dawn comes at last. Hat Man is early today. 'It is a busy day for me,' says Hat Man, 'so all you creatures are out early too.' He lets out the geese, and then he lets out Cow. Then the goats. And at last he opens the door of the sheep house. Out come Woolly and all his friends onto the soft green grass. Woolly sees me by the food bucket. He winks his pale eye.

Hat Man turns to go. 'See you later!' says he. In a moment he is gone round the corner of the shed and away into the far side of the farm.

Woolly watches Hat Man until he is gone from sight. Then he turns and stares around the sheep pen. The sheep pen is big and square. There is a high fence all round it. The fence has three big bars and between the bars is netting to stop the lambs when they are small.

'Up and over,' says Woolly Woolly Baa Lamb. 'That is the only way.'

'You cannot do it,' I say. 'That bar is as high as your ears. You are brave and you are strong but that fence is too high.'

'Watch me!' says Woolly.

He looks round once more for Hat Man. Then he starts to run. He starts to trot. Round the inside of the fence.

Of course his other sheep friends are there. They

stare. They move out of his way. They bunch together in the middle of the paddock.

'What are you doing, friend Woolly?' they ask him.

He does not reply.

He trots on around the fence. His hard hooves hit the ground like hammers. They throw up little slices of mud as he goes. His head is high. His eyes gleam blue as the sky.

Once, twice, three times he trots around the square. He goes faster and faster. Thud thud go his hard hooves. 'Haah! Haah!' goes his breath through his tight white nose.

Suddenly he spins on his back feet. He bunches his round shoulders. He bends his heavy thighs. He leaps.

Lambs and sheep jump high. They do. They are famous for it. But never has lambkin leapt like Woolly does this bright morning.

Up he goes into the air. His four feet stretch out behind him. His round white body flies upwards. It floats, it hangs in the air. Up, up he goes. To the top of the fence. To the high bar.

Almost.

He has not jumped high enough. His knees hit the bar. He crunches down upon it, half one side, half the other. The sharp wood hits into his round white belly.

'Oooooah!!' goes Woolly. All the air is pushed out of him.

He strikes out with his front hooves against the wood. His back feet kick and kick into the empty air. He is stuck. He sways this way and that on the high wooden bar.

I put my paws up to my ratty ears. 'Oh Woolly,' I cry. 'Brave Woolly. Who can help you now?'

There is the thud of sharp hooves behind me. His sheep friends have come up close. They peer and stare and nod their sheep heads. 'We can help you!' they bleat. 'We are your friends, Woolly. We will help you!'

They pull back a little. They stamp their sharp front hooves. And then they come.

They come. Not in ones and twos but all together. All the sheep together. A wall of white and speckled wool.

Trot, trot, they go upon their pointed hooves. Down go their heads. They trot, they gallop forward. All together. They reach the fence. Up they jump, all together. They crash their heads forward, all together. In a single stroke.

31

Up goes Woolly. Over goes Woolly. Up and over and forward like a woolly bird.

He skims through the air. He lands on his four hard hooves a long space from that high fence.

He turns slowly. He turns and he smiles. His eyes are gentle, which is rare for Woolly. 'Friends,' says he, 'dear friends. Thank you, thank you.'

The sheep wave their ears politely. 'Off you go now,' they say. 'Wherever you are going, you had better be quick. We will try to stop Hat Man noticing, for as long as we are able.'

'I will tell you all about it when I get back,' says Woolly. 'Now Ratty, up you get and off we go!'

I leap forward and scramble up his curly front leg. He is not so high and comfy as Cow to ride on. But there is lots of wool to cling to, so he is safe and sure.

'We must get out of here,' hisses Woolly. He glances round the farm.

No sign of Hat Man yet. No sign of Cow neither. And that is odd. She must have heard the noise, that is what I think. She must be watching us from the dark shadows of her cowhouse. What is Cow thinking? I wish I knew.

But there is no time for wondering. It is time for off! Out of the farm goes Woolly, with me upon his back. Rat tat tat go his hooves as he trots through the farm gate. Rat tat tat along the road we go.

It is early. There is no one about, but in the distance we hear the first sounds of cars and buses. We must get away and out of sight. Then Woolly stops. He skips sideways. He slips under a broken fence at the roadside. And here we are! On the side of the railway bank. A muddy track stretches ahead of us through the brambles.

'I hope we don't go near the trains!' I squeak. My ears stand straight up with terror. Trains. They are huge and loud and fierce. They make the ground shake.

'Ratty!' says Woolly over his shoulder. 'I am a sensible sheep you know. I do not want to be a sheep rug. We will not go near the railway line. And anyway, if you look you will see there is a big fence.'

Up I peer and he is right. 'Phew!' says I. 'I am glad of that. I am sorry, Woolly. Sometimes I am a foolish ratty. I trust you. I do.'

'I shall go along the bottom of this bank,' says Woolly. 'It is thick and bushy and no one will see us. It should take us all the way to where we are going.'

'Wherever that may be,' I whisper to myself. I lay my brown head upon his soft and woolly shoulder. I push my claws tight into his wool. I fall asleep.

Woolly trots on. Even in my sleep I can tell it is hard going. Brambles and thorns pull at Woolly's coat. They catch at his feet. He pushes and trips and jumps. There is no path now. And all the time above our heads the railway line lies cold and still.

Then I hear a new noise. I am awake in half a breath. The two steel lines above us hum, high and soft.

'A train is coming,' says Woolly. 'We must hide.' Down he drops, under a thorn bush. Down and flat until he looks like a white rough stone on the green bank.

Whistle. Rattle. Roar. Closer. Louder. I bury my head in Woolly's thick coat. I pull wool over my round ears.

Crash!

The train is over and past us. Crash and rattle and roar. Away it goes again. Quieter. Quieter. Until all that is left is the dying hum of the railway lines.

'There will be more,' says Woolly. 'We must get on.' He climbs up onto his feet and steps forward once more.

'What are we looking for?' I ask.

'The blue-ring sheep of course,' says Woolly. 'They are next to the railway line. We know that. We will go on until we find them!'

Well that is that. It sounds so easy. But will it work? I am not sure it will but I do not say a word. Woolly is sure and that will have to do.

It is a long way. A long way. The sun rises higher and higher. It shines bright upon us. We stop while Woolly eats and rests as he must. Trains pass and each time we hide. But on we go. The city is far behind us now.

Green fields stretch on every side.

At last ahead of us we see a farmhouse. It is three fields from the railway line. Close by the railway bank stands a barn.

Woolly stops. I stare. We see sheep. Sheep, in this field, and the next field, and the next. Sheep, as far as my ratty eyes can see.

'Look!' I whisper in Woolly's ear. 'Look there, Woolly my friend.'

On the back of every sheep there is a clear blue circle. Blue-ring sheep as far as my sharp ratty eyes can see. We have found the place. Just in time too. The sun is moving down the sky. The shadows are long and dark.

'Food time,' says Woolly. Straight down the bank he goes towards the green flat fields. Down he slides like a cannon ball. I hang on tight as tight. I close my eyes. Whump. We land at the bottom.

I open my eyes. Woolly's nose is pressed hard against a wire fence. 'I cannot jump this,' says he.

There is a sudden scuffle of sharp hooves. I look up. Right in front of us is a grey sheep. She has a long face and bright eyes.

'You can't jump it,' says she. 'But you do not need to. Trot that way and there's a sheep door, neat as neat. Where there's a sheep there's a way,' says she.

Off we trot and there it is. The wire fence has been pushed up at the bottom by strong sheep shoulders. Underneath is a scooped hollow of earth dug out by sharp sheep hooves.

'We like the green shoots on that bank,' says the sheep from the field. 'We make sure we get them. Come on through.' It is a wide gap and Woolly is through it quick as a flash.

'Well,' says the sheep, 'I've got some eating to do before the dark so I'll be off.' Away she trots to munch the short grass. That is Woolly's idea too. He bends his head and opens his hard little mouth. Then munch munch munch he goes like a machine. It is no use talking to him now. He will eat and eat. Then he will chew and chew.

I curl up at the bottom of a thorn tree. I go to sleep. I think that I am safe.

I am a town ratty now you must remember. I have forgot what once I knew when I lived at Farmer's farm. You will say I am a stupid ratty, and you will be right.

So I snooze and doze as peaceful as can be as if there are no creatures in the world who like a ratty snack. I snooze until, as morning dawns, I feel a soft breath on my fur. Is it a breeze?

I look up. No!

It is hot breath from a killing mouth. Right above me.

I am awake before my heart hits out another beat.

I know what this is. I know whose mouth I see. This is a red foxy throat and these are white foxy teeth. Reaching out for me.

Ready to eat me up.

CHAPTER 4

I stare up into that red and open mouth for just a heartbeat.

Then I leap sideways.

I somersault. I dive under a heavy stone at the tree root.

'Oh Foxy Loxy!' says I. My voice shakes. My whiskers tremble. 'Foxy Loxy. My heart has almost stopped. You will be the death of me.'

'I hope so,' says Foxy Loxy. 'That is my plan.' She peers down at me over her sharp russet nose.

'No no!' says I. 'I am not breakfast or tea. I am a cunning creature like yourself. I am a friend and not a meal, dear Foxy,' says I.

She sits back and wraps her beautiful red tail around her. 'Mmmm,' say she. 'Good try, Ratty. But how is a hungry fox to feed herself? She cannot leave fat round ratties to live whole in their skins.'

I do not like this talk. I stroke my furry skin. I stroke my round fat belly. They are me. I do not want them chopped up in Foxy's insides.

'Think again,' says I. 'I am not snoozing here for fun. I am on a mission. An adventure. My friend and I are here to save the pups.'

At this she sits up indeed. Her eyes go round and startled. Her ears flick back and forth. She opens her pointed mouth and stares at me. 'You know about the pups?' says she. 'How so?'

I tell her. As I speak she leans her head and listens and nods. She does not look so much like a ratty-eater now I think.

'I will not eat you Ratty,' says she. 'I am glad you have come. I hear the pups each day. Of course they are only doggo pups and not my lovely cublets. But they should not be locked up so. I will help you if I can.'

I stick my nose out from my stone shelter. I hope she speaks the truth. I point with my front paw across the field. The sheep are waking now and the dew sparkles on the grass.

'That is my friend, over there,' says I. 'He is called Woolly Woolly Baa Lamb. He is a hero.'

'He will need to be,' says Foxy Loxy.

Suddenly she is stiff on her four paws. She turns her head. She sniffs the breeze. Before I can blink she is gone.

Over the field I hear the tramp tramp of heavy feet.

People feet. Then I see them. Two men tramping over the field towards us. In one wink of my eye I know them. Jeth and Tone.

'Hey Tone,' calls Jeth. 'We've got a new one here!'

He has found Woolly.

Woolly has slept deep. He is not so wide awake as he needs to be. He is lying on the morning grass, white as a heap of chalk. There is no blue ring on him.

'Hello, hello,' says Tone in his squeaky voice. 'What a fat little lambkin we've got here, Jeth! What a chubby chap!'

'Yes indeed,' growls Jeth. 'Chubby and tasty too, I'm sure!' He chuckles. It is a nasty sound.

'Lots of little lamb chops in you my dear,' giggles Tone, 'and some nice stew for Jeth and me. A roast or two as well I'll be bound.'

'I wonder where he came from?' says Jeth. 'But then,' says he, 'do we care?'

They both laugh loud again.

'What a nice pressy he is,' says Tone. 'And he's come all on his own-some to see us. How nice. Never look a gift sheep in the mouth – that is what I say.'

'He needs his little marker, don't he now!' growls Jeth.

'Very true,' says Tone.

Quick as a flash they both lunge forward. Jeth seizes Woolly's right ear. Tone grabs Woolly's left ear. They heave him to his feet.

'Oooow!' cries Woolly. 'Oooow and ooow again!'

It is no use.

'This way,' says Jeth.

They keep hold of Woolly's two ears. They turn and trudge back across the field to the barn. Woolly goes with them. He has to.

I see him go. I see him cross the field and go out through the gate. I see him cross the track and step into the barn. I see the dark door close behind him.

I sit back under my tree. I lean against the cold trunk.

I am alone. All alone.

I stare ahead over the field. Then I blink and stare again. In front of me are white and speckled sheep. Everywhere. But there is something else.

In the middle of the field. Something very big. White yes, and speckled too. But not a sheep. I do not think it is a sheep.

It is coming this way.

I have had enough frights for one day. I should hide under the stone. Of course I should. But I do not. I just sit and I wait.

The white thing comes closer. It stops in front of me. It lowers its white head. Its huge white head.

It sniffs. I grab a tree root and hold on tight. One sniff and away I could go. It has nostrils as big as my

head. Bigger. They are soft and round and bendy at the edges. A soft breath sweeps over me. It smells of warm hay.

I lift my eyes. I stare up at a long and bony face. I see two dark eyes with lashes white as snow. I see two pointed ears turned towards me. And a tangled plume of hair that falls forward over that long nose.

'Horse,' I whisper. 'Horse!'

I have never seen Horse before. I have heard stories of course. How strong, how swift, how tall. But never in my ratty life have I seen one.

I look at her feet. Horse feet are different, that I know. Feet like stones. Round and grey and hard. 'Watch out for feet,' I think.

I look up again at the long face. 'Horse?' I say out loud.

'Yes, Horse,' says she. 'White Horse.' She tosses her

head up high and stamps her foot.

'Oh no!' thinks I. One stamp from that foot and I would be a round flat rattyo and breathe no more. I lean back against my tree trunk as far as I can go.

'I saw you come in last night,' says she. 'I saw them take your friend just now. They have shut him up.'

I nod.

'Let's go,' says White Horse. 'Let us go and help him.'

I stare again. What does she mean?

'Up! Up!' she says. 'Onto my shoulder. Let us see what we can do. Not scared I hope?'

Scared? Of course I am! Scared and shaking too.

'Hup!' says she again.

Well, I have climbed onto Cow's horned head. I have climbed onto Woolly's curly back. But how can I climb up to this high white shoulder?

But I must. If White Horse can help Woolly, I must.

So out I leap from under my tree. I reach up. She lowers her neck. The tangled hair of her mane brushes the grass. I grab it. I swing up and stand at last upon her curved shoulder. Now I am up I see that she is not white at all but covered in silver rings like frost. She shines in the sun. A silver horse.

I wrap my paws in the thick strands of her mane. I cling tight.

I am so high. So high. The blue swallows fly around my head. The ground is far below.

'Oh Horse,' I say. 'Is this Heaven? So high. So far from ground.'

'Not Heaven yet,' says she. 'Hold on tight!'

She turns from the high fence, which looks low now. She paces forward. I seize her mane with tighter claws. I stare ahead between her pointed ears.

She paces. She begins to trot upon her long legs. For a step or two. Then she reaches forward and she begins to run. She runs like a river. Like the wind. Like otter flowing through his cold stream. Like hawk in the high air.

The wind blows over us. The green grass skims past us. Her hooves thud and drum upon the ground. Her long back stretches and sways. She pours around that field. I, Ratty, cling and gasp.

'This is Heaven. Now is Heaven,' I cry into the wind.

And then I start to sing. I sing. Never before, never again perhaps. But here and now I sing.

Horse turns her pointed ears. She smiles.

And runs on.

Then she bunches her shoulders and curves her neck and pulls her back short. And stops.

I cling tight and laugh for joy.

'Dear Horse,' says I, 'if I could run like that I would never stop.'

'Dear Ratty,' says she, 'you would, you know. You would stop for food, for quiet times, for sleep. And when you had work to do. Here we are by the barn. We must rescue your friend. So what do we do now?'

White Horse is standing at a wooden fence. Just in front of us is the high dark shape of the barn. There is a square of hard ground in front of it with grass growing through it. A stony track leads away on either side. One way goes to the farmhouse in the distance, the other way into the fields.

I stare again at the barn. At this end it has doors, big doors. I do not think they have been opened for a long while. The grass grows high against them. Perhaps they will not open now.

There is another way in. A door is cut for people into one of the panels. It is an ordinary opening door and it is fastened with a piece of string.

I have looked enough. I lift my brown nose and I

sniff. I sniff and sniff again. The air tells me what I want to know.

'Oh Horse,' says I, 'that place is full of doggos. I can smell them. More doggos than I have ever seen in one place.'

White Horse nods her big head. 'You are right about the doggos,' says she. 'I hear them sometimes. We never see them. They don't come out you know. Except to go away in the blue van. And that is in the night-time always.' She looks troubled. 'Now your friend is in there,' says she.

'Yes,' says I. 'I smell him too.'

Woolly is there, that is what my nose tells me. And he is cross. I smell his crossness. My heart skips a little. All is not lost while Woolly is angry.

'I must find out more,' says I. 'I will slide down if I may. I need to look around.'

'Of course,' says Horse. 'I will wait for you here.'

I slide off her back and leap down onto the stony track.

'Thank you White Horse,' says I. 'I will be back soon I hope.'

I bound forward over the dry hard ground. My claws make little scratchy noises as I go. Now I am close, I see the barn is made of metal. Old and rusty metal. That is good news for me. If metal is rusty, it will have holes in it. That is a ratty fact – I know it.

I scuttle off around the barn corner and stop. The barn is huge. From where I stand on my short legs I

cannot see the end of it. All along the side there are cracks and splits and holes. I creep along until I find a hole that is a comfy rat size. Through I pop.

It takes a moment for my eyes to see, so dark it is.

When I can see, I stare and shake my head and stare again. It is a strange sight indeed.

In every shadowed corner I see machines. Silent, resting, sleeping. Tractors, diggers, an old car, a plough. All lying still. All laced with spiders' webs.

At one end the barn roof is torn back and gaping to the sky. Chill air blows in. This is a cold bad place. Not a good place for ratties, nor for pups neither.

I listen.

I hear the snort of an angry sheep. Woolly is at the end of the barn, next to the door. That is good news.

But what is here in front of me?

In the middle of the barn is a high square shape. It is a wall of straw. I understand! It is a wall to keep pups in. And maybe shelter them in this cold place. A wall of straw bales. And it has a gate like walls do. Not an ordinary gate but a gap covered with soft squared mesh.

I can see through. And what I see is pups. More pups than I have ever seen in all my life or dreams. They lie all heaped and snoring in the dim light. Here and there a head pushes up and yawns. A shoulder moves. A tail.

'Oh my,' says I, 'fifty pups at least. And each one with sharp teeth to chew a ratty!' But then I watch on and see that they wobble when they walk. These pups are very young. Perhaps their teeth are still too small to bite with.

The pups begin to stir. It is breakfast time. 'Food!' they yelp. 'Where is it? Food! Now!' They are too small and weak to climb out of their pen. So they yelp and whine and howl and look towards the barn door.

Perhaps the men will be back soon to feed them. I must go to find Woolly.

I scurry down the barn towards the door. Then I see him. He is standing sad and still in a circle of fence near the barn door.

Two leaps and I am there beside him.

'Hello, dear Woolly,' says I.

Woolly spins on his plump back legs. His eyes gleam to see me. For just a second. Then he slumps his round shoulders and droops his round neck.

'Ratty!' says he. 'I hoped so much that you would find me. But Ratty, they have got me now!'

He turns his back to me. I see a blue circle set bright and new upon his broad back. 'They have got me now,' says Woolly Woolly Baa Lamb. 'No one will believe I am a free Woolly now. I am one of theirs!'

He opens his hard white mouth. He bleats to the high roof. His voice is sad and frightened. But all the time his tail goes twitch, twitch, twitch. Woolly is angry in his heart.

'Me!' he bleats. He stamps his foot and looks at me so hard that his eyes cross. 'They steal me as if I was a parcel! They will see,' says Woolly in a fierce whisper. 'They will see.'

Just then there is a scuffle close behind me. A scuffle, and the sound of panting breath.

I spin around. There behind me stands a pup. He pushes forward into Woolly's pen and stares at me with round eyes. I stare back.

The pup is white and black in patches. Stiff hairs have started to grow through his soft puppy down. He is no baby like the others. He does not wobble or whine. He is quick and fierce, with eyes like needles.

'My name is Nip,' says he. 'Little Dog Nip. My teeth are sharp and if I were bigger I would eat you up!'

'I think you would!' says I. 'I know a ratty-catcher

when I see one. But now you are too small and anyway I am your friend.'

'I met Woolly this morning,' says Nip. 'And now I meet you. Perhaps the world is more exciting than I thought.'

'It is too exciting by half,' says I.

Then Crash! Smash! The door in the barn end cracks open. Thump! In steps Jeth and in steps Tone.

Little Dog Nip wags his tail and bounces off towards the two men. I am away under the straw and out of sight before a spider can blink its eye.

The other pups lift their heads when they hear the men. 'Yap Yap!' they go. 'Breakfast time!'

Jeth steps over to the straw wall and leans to look at them. 'Well, well,' says he, 'How are our little pounds and dollars today? How are our little money-spinners this bright morning?' He peers at the pups with a smile all over his flinty face.

Tone comes over to take a look at Woolly. 'And how is our woolly friend here?' says he. 'What nice lamb chops you will make.' He slaps his hand on Woolly's broad back. He is lucky not to get Woolly's hard head in his middle.

Then the two men go to get the puppy food. I do not wait. Out I go. Out through the nearest crack into the sun-filled world outside.

I stand and sniff the clear clean air.

Then I look around for White Horse. She is waiting near the fence. She is eating. She tears up the grass with a noise I can hear from the barn side. She lifts her head in mid-bite as she sees me. Two flashes of her big yellow teeth and down the mouthful goes. I scuttle over to where she stands.

'Ratty,' says she, 'you do not have a happy face. Did you find your friend?'

I sit back on my plump haunches and peer up at her. 'He is there,' I say, 'and frightened too. Those men are bad men.' I frown. 'The barn is full of pups. I do not understand why the men need so many. And now Woolly is with them. We must save Woolly. He is my friend.'

'Of course we must save him,' says White Horse. 'So let us think how. If you climb up we can find a quiet corner to think in.'

I reach for Horse's mane. I scramble up the strands of rough hair. I sit upon her broad and silver back. And off we trot across the green field.

I think of Woolly in his cold prison and I sigh. Then I lift my head and look between Horse's pointed ears.

I look and then I stare.

There is something new in the field. Something that is not grey or white like sheep.

Something black and white.

CHAPTER 5

I stare and stare again.

'Cow!' I squeak. I almost tumble from my high seat. There she is. Right by the fence. Munching the green grass. Calm as can be.

'Oh White Horse,' I whisper into Horse's ear. 'Strong and mighty Horse. Over there is my dearest oldest friend. Let us go to her quickly!'

Horse rears up upon her strong back legs. She plunges forward across the field. The grass thuds beneath her feet.

We are there faster than the wind.

Cow hears us coming. She lifts her patterned head. And smiles. And whisks her tail. As if it is ordinary time and all as it should be.

Horse skids to a halt. Cow looks at us and goes on chewing.

'Cow! Dear Cow!' I squeak. I lean forward from

Horse's high shoulder. 'Dear Cow. It is so good to see you. Why are you here? How did you get out of the Farm?'

'Dear Ratty friend,' says Cow. She gives a little skip of joy. 'It is so grand to be here and out and free.' She looks at White Horse. 'I am pleased to meet you,' says she and nods her head.

Horse smiles her slow horse smile.

'But how did you get here?' I squeak. 'Please tell me, Cow. I did not think you could escape. How did it happen?'

'Chee helped me,' says she. 'She went and found Mousy and all her family. Together they got me out!'

'But how?' I squeak.

'Well, Hat Man helped too,' says Cow, 'though he did not mean to. He was so upset when Woolly disappeared. He got in a muddle and then Chee muddled him more by barking and barking. So he did not shut my door quite right. The mousy family pushed and pulled the bolt and got it open easy beasy. I walked out oh so quiet while Hat Man finished cleaning. It was almost dark you know,' says she. 'No one saw me.'

She nods her head sadly. 'Hat Man will be more upset than ever now that I am gone too.'

I have nothing to say to that. It is not good but what else could she do? 'But Cow,' says I, 'how did you get here? It is a long way.'

'Like you,' says she. 'I saw where you went, along the high bank. And I came the same way. Then through the fence like you. It was hard for one as big as me, but I did it and I am here now! But Ratty,' says she, lifting her head and looking round the field. 'Where is Woolly? I cannot see him.'

I twist my little paws together. 'Dear Cow,' says I, 'the bad men have got Woolly. That is the truth. He is trapped in the barn with the pups. It has all gone wrong. And now it will be even worse. You are here and the bad men will get you as well. I know they will. Oh Cow!' I squeak.

Cow's eyes open wide. 'They have got Woolly! How sad! But Ratty friend, do not despair. There is you and me and White Horse too. We can save them all!'

White Horse bends her long neck forward. 'We must rescue Woolly first. That is what I think,' says she. 'Then four of us together can help the pups you know.'

'How can Woolly get out?' says Cow. 'What must we do?'

'There is a little door in the barn end,' I explain to Cow. 'It is fastened tight with a string. If we could undo that we might rescue him.'

'String?' says Cow. 'I am no good at string.'

Horse shakes her big head sadly. 'Nor me with my big hooves,' says she. 'Who can reach high and undo string? Who can help us?'

I stare up into the bright sky. Over our heads the swallows skim on their long wings. They snap flies out of the air. They circle, they loop, they turn.

'I know,' I whisper. 'I think I know. May I stand on the top of your head, White Horse?' I ask. 'Just for a moment?'

She nods. So up I go. It is a hard scramble up her neck. Her mane juts out like a thick hedge. I crawl and push and at last I stand between her ears. I wrap the long hairs round my front paws.

Then I lean back. I stare into the sky. I call out in my high ratty voice, as loud as I am able.

'Swallows!' I cry. 'Swallow friends! Hear me!' Above my head they tunnel through the air with mouths agape. 'Swallows!' I call again. 'Help me!'

Many are so high they cannot hear me. But one does. There is a rush of air and here he is, right next to Horse's ears. His back gleams blue like the night. He hovers in front of me like a huge butterfly.

'You want help?' says he.

'Yes please,' says I. 'My friend is shut in the barn. There is a knot to be undone or else he is shut in for ever.'

Swallow shoots up into the air with a clap of his blue wings.

'Shut in!' he calls as he tunnels upwards into the wind. His voice drifts down the air to me. 'No one can shut us in. No one.'

Then suddenly he is back. 'Where is this string?' says he.

I turn and speak into Horse's silver ear. 'Come Horse if you will,' I say, 'and we can show this kind bird the very place.'

Then I turn to Cow. 'Please Cow stay here in this corner,' says I. 'The track is over that side of the field. If the men come they may not see you if you stay here.' Cow nods her head and sighs. She would like to come and help rescue Woolly but she knows she must be sensible.

'Now Horse,' I whisper.

Horse lifts her great feet and off she trots. No more galloping for us. And all the while Swallow skims about our heads.

We reach the fence. We reach the track side. I point with my brown paw.

'There is the door,' I say. 'There is the string.'

Swallow is off – a blue flash that skims past the door and is back before I blink.

'Easy,' says he. 'A thread here, a thread there. We will help you, me and my friends. Watch us! Watch us!' He claps his wings close. He shoots forward towards the door. Snip goes his beak.

Past me flashes another blue shape. Snip goes another beak. Then another. And another.

The swallows swoop by us like bullets from Farmer's gun. They skim past the door. Then soar up into the high air. And every time one more thread is snipped away.

Then Snip! The last thread is cut.

Clang! The door swings open.

Blue Swallow skims back. He hovers for just a second over my head. His mouth is full of dry threads.

'Your friend can run free now,' says he through the bristling threads. 'Like us. Like us.'

He turns and shoots up into the heights and is lost to my eye.

The door swings gently on its rusty hinges.

'White Horse,' says I, 'now it is time to free Woolly!'

'No time like now,' says White Horse.

So I seize her strong mane and down I slide. Then off I bound across the stony ground. The door is swinging open. With one leap in I go.

The dark closes round me. But there in the gloom I see Woolly's pale face staring back at me.

'Ratty,' says he. 'The door! The door is open!'

'Yes it is,' says I. 'And you must run straight out through it. There is only your fencing here in the way.'

'This fence is nothing to me. Watch now!' cries Woolly.

He puts down his head and stamps his feet. Straight through the fence he goes like a bullet. The bits fly up into the air and fall about him like rain.

He is a new Woolly now. Or rather he is the old

Woolly. He is like he was before. No more fright. No more sadness. His blue eyes flash.

'Now out I go,' says Woolly, 'and who will stop me?'

'Let us be quick,' says I, 'or someone may try!'

Woolly has not waited. Trot trot he goes across the hard floor. He thrusts his head out of the swinging door. He looks this way and that. Then out he leaps and disappears into the sunshine, leaving the dark behind.

And me after him.

Here we are, the two of us, side by side in the bright air.

Woolly's eyes flick here and there. Suddenly he sees White Horse. 'Oomph!' says he in a quiet sort of voice. 'Who is that there, Ratty? What is that? It is so big, so strong. Do you know that creature there?'

'Indeed I do,' says I. 'That is White Horse. She is a new friend and she will help us. Come and meet her now.'

Woolly cheers up at this. He trots over to the high fence. Horse lowers her great head. They sniff noses carefully.

'Welcome,' says Horse.

'I am glad to meet you,' says Woolly. 'What a big new friend you are.' He stares up at her high speckled shoulder. 'You are almost sheep colour,' says he, 'and that is a good colour to be.'

White Horse smiles. Then she goes serious. 'You must hide,' says she. 'There is just one place for a sheep to hide and that is in a sheep field. You must get over this fence,' says White Horse.

The fence is high and it is strong. Woolly waves his ears at it for a moment. Then he shakes his head.

'No,' says he. 'I have to be on your side of the fence but I do not have to get over it. Wait!' He spins on his back hooves and off he trots. Round behind the barn.

White Horse stares and so do I. There is no sign of Woolly now. Then suddenly I see him.

'Over there!' I squeak to Horse. Woolly is on the railway bank. He is trotting through the bushes as calm as can be. He disappears again where the sheep hole is. Then from the middle of the field we hear his voice.

'All safe and sheep-shape now!' bleats Woolly. He starts to sing in a high and reedy voice.

'I am a blue-ring sheep
a blue-ring sheep
a blue-ring sheep,
I am a blue-ring sheep
And who can find me now!'

He dances a little bouncing dance in the green centre of the field. The sheep about him stare and wag their tails and munch on.

'Who can find me now?' sings Woolly. He settles back upon his four hooves and smiles on all the world.

Woolly is safe and Woolly is hidden, right in the middle of the wide green field.

I scramble up onto White Horse's shoulder. She makes her way across the field, stepping carefully through the eating sheep. As we get nearer Woolly laughs up at us in the morning sun.

'Lost in the crowd – that's me,' says he. 'How good to be free and with my friends once more!'

Behind him I see Cow, trotting across the field towards us. I must tell him that she is here. Or what a shock he will get!

'Oh Woolly!' I cry. 'You have more friends than you think. There is something I must tell you!'

'Something to tell me?' says Woolly. 'I have something to tell you. I am a brave lamb,' says Woolly. 'I am a lamb of steel. But those two bad men make me tremble.'

'Dear Woolly,' says Cow's voice from behind him. 'We know how brave you are.'

Woolly goes pale as frost. He shakes like a leaf in a high breeze. He stands stiff on his four legs and stares ahead of him.

'Ratty,' says he. 'I thought I heard Cow. But that cannot be. I know she is so far away. Is it a ghost? Or some other creepy thing, pretending to be Cow? Or am I hearing things! What is happening?' says he. Then he closes his eyes.

He stands there. Pale and shaking and not a hero lamb at all.

'Turn round,' says I. 'You are hearing true things, that is what. Do not fret woolly friend. Cow is here,

her very self. Real Cow, true Cow. And if you turn round you will see her.'

Woolly turns slow as slow. When he is right round, he opens one eye, just a tiny bit, then more, then more. Then he opens the other eye. A smile breaks out upon his hard sheep face. 'Oh Cow,' he bleats. 'How good to see you!'

But suddenly he frowns. 'Ratty,' says he. 'Is Cow safe here? What will the bad men do?'

I shake my head. 'Cow is not safe at all,' says I. 'She is so big and there is nowhere to hide her. Oh dear, oh dear,' says I.

White Horse turns her long head round to look at me perched upon her back. She blows a breath out of her soft nostrils. 'Do not worry Ratty. There are lots of things to think about,' says she. 'But first we should rest awhile. I need to eat and I am sure that you would like a snack, Woolly.'

'Oh yes indeed,' says Woolly. This is his kind of talk.

'There is some long grass in that corner,' says Cow. 'That will suit me. Then if the men come I shall lie down and the grass will hide me.'

I slide down from Horse's high back. White Horse follows Cow into the deep grass in the field corner. Soon they are pulling and chewing and swallowing like two big harvester machines.

I find a sunny spot next to a fence post. I doze. Woolly bites at the shorter grass with his sharp teeth. The sun shines down upon us. It is a peaceful scene.

There is a soft rustle from the bank. I open one eye. Here comes Foxy Loxy trotting through the sheep hole into the field. She is licking her lips. Someone has gone the snip-snap way into her red insides but I will not think of that.

Foxy Loxy blinks a bit when she sees Cow. I call out from my warm grass bed. 'This is Cow, Foxy Loxy. She is my oldest friend in all the world. We are resting awhile and then we will think about the pups.'

Foxy Loxy nods to Cow. Cow smiles and chews on. Foxy settles down upon the warm grass. She half shuts her golden eyes.

Woolly plumps down upon the ground and gives a sigh. 'Escaping is hard work,' says he. Then he closes his blue eyes and stretches out his bony legs. Soon he is breathing slow and deep and snoozing like a good lamb should.

I close my eyes again. At last I sleep while Horse and Cow tear and munch at the soft green grass.

Cow is a clever cow. She can chew the long grass and flap her big ears and think, all at the same time. That is what she does while I doze.

'Does the farmer know about the pups?' she asks at last.

I sit up smartish. I want to hear this. Woolly wakes up too.

'No,' says White Horse after one more chew. 'Farmer lets those two men have the barn. They do his work around the farm. Farmer is not a bad man,' says White

Horse. 'But he is busy. He does not come this way except to check his sheep. And to bring me apples.'

'If Farmer cares about his sheep, he must be good enough,' says Woolly. 'But those two men are bad enough for anything.'

'I do not understand why the men want so many puppies,' says Cow.

'They sell them!' says I. I am wide awake now. 'Remember Pup! He was taken to be sold. I do not understand it all but somehow selling pups and getting money is what the bad men do.'

'What should we do?' says Cow. 'Please Ratty, tell us what you think.'

'We came to save the pups, of course we did,' says I. 'But they are very small you know. They cannot walk far I am sure.'

Cow is worried. 'We must find a warm dry place to take them. The City Farm would be the best but it is far away.' She shakes her head. 'It is not sensible,' says she. 'We must be careful. They are only babies you know.'

My heart is wobbling in my chest. I fear that Cow is right. It is not sensible. What can we do?

Just then Horse lifts her white head. Her tall ears flick this way and that.

'The tractor!' says she. 'The men are coming!'

Well that is that. The end of talking.

'Oh Cow, this way! Into the corner!' neighs Horse. 'I can stand in front of you and hide you.'

Cow is not a fast mover. Never was. But into that corner she pushes fast enough to make me blink. Then down she goes. Slowly. Of course. That is what cows do. First her front legs. Then her back ones. And all the time I hear the growling roar of the tractor coming closer. Closer.

At last Cow is down. The long grass waves about her.

'You will have to get your head down, Cow!' bleats Woolly. 'What a big head you have!'

'I cannot help that now!' says Cow. She sounds cross but I see her stretch her neck out until her head is flat amongst the green grass stalks. Only the tips of her horns show now. And who will see those from the distant track?

'Oh Cow. Dear clever Cow,' I whisper. 'Perhaps you will be safe.'

White Horse stands big and tall in front of Cow's dark shape. She whisks her horsy tail and shakes her horsy head and takes up as much room as she can.

'I will trot off amongst my blue-ring friends,' says Woolly. Off he skips singing under his breath very quiet,

> *'I am a blue-ring sheep*
> *a blue-ring sheep*
> *a blue-ring sheep!*
> *I am a blue-ring sheep*
> *and who can find me now!'*

Cow is being flat. Horse is being as big as a horse can be. And Woolly is being a blue-ring sheep.

So what do I do?

I run, quick as a brown shadow to the track side. I crouch low behind a thick wooden fence post. I hide. And I listen.

CHAPTER 6

I crouch by my fence post. I listen and I look. Here comes the tractor bouncing along the track. Perched on the top are Jeth and Tone.

Tone stares at the door. Then he blinks and stares again. He pulls Jeth's arm.

'Hey Jeth,' squeaks Tone. 'Is that door meant to be open?'

'What!' yells Jeth. The tractor slams to a stop. 'What!'

He stares too. 'Oh Tone my lad,' cries Jeth, 'there's mischief here.' He is down from the tractor seat quicker than a rabbit down a hole.

He stares at the swinging door. He stares at the place where the string should be. 'Where is the string?' he whispers to himself. 'Where has it gone? No sign at all.' He shakes his heavy head.

'Are the pups still there?' asks Tone.

Jeth takes a lunge in through that dark door. A moment later I hear him roar, 'The pups are here. Yes they are. But I will tell you who is gone. That fat lambkin! That little roast on the bone. Gone and not a curl left!'

He roars so loud that Woolly hears him where he is standing safe in the middle of the field. Woolly shakes his head and stamps his hoof. 'I am not fat,' says he. 'I am sturdy. And a nice lambkin shape it is too.'

Jeth is getting crosser and crosser. 'That lamb is off and gone!' says Jeth. He steps out of the barn door and glares about him. His hands are on his hips. His face is red.

'Did the lambkin eat the door string then?' asks Tone.

'Do not be stupid!' howls Jeth. 'How could he eat it through the door? No, my boy, there's been someone helping him there has. Mischief that's what. Mischief! And our friend did not tell us!'

Friend? Who is Jeth's friend? That is what I wonder. But there is no time for wondering now.

Jeth reaches into his pocket. Out comes a chain with a lock hanging from it. 'It is Farmer's chain, I know,' says he, 'but it is more use here than on Farmer's shed.' In two clicks the door is tight shut again.

'Now Tone,' says he, 'let us be on our way or Farmer will be chasing us. I don't like this at all.' He shakes his head crossly.

'But it is all fine now,' says Tone. 'No one can shift that lock, I am sure.'

'Fine! What can you mean?' howls Jeth. 'Someone has been into our barn. They have pinched our sheep! They have seen our pups! They have got away and talked to who knows who! What is fine about that?'

Tone stares at Jeth. His face is blank as blank. 'Oh dear,' says he. 'Perhaps we are in trouble still.'

'Of course we are in trouble!' yells Jeth. 'We must move those pups as quick as winking.' He scratches his head and frowns. 'I do not think we can move them today. But tomorrow they must go – or the day after. Then, when the pups are gone, we will be in the clear!' He climbs slowly back onto the high tractor.

Tone nods his head. 'You are a clever thinker Jeth,' says he. 'You will sort us out.'

'You are not the only clever thinker around here,' I whisper behind my fence post.

The tractor roars and turns and jolts off along the track.

Off I go. Quick as a brown shadow back across the field.

Here is Horse, standing tall and waving her long tail. Cow is getting up from being a cow pancake. Foxy Loxy comes out from the bushes where she hid away. Woolly comes trotting back across the field.

They stare at me with all their eight eyes. 'Well?' says Foxy Loxy.

'What is happening?' asks Cow.

'Tell us Ratty!' bleats Woolly.

'Is there news?' says White Horse gently.

'There is. There is,' I squeak. 'And bad news too. The pups will be moved. Tomorrow! It may be tomorrow! We have no time at all. We must rescue them straight away!'

'Hurrah!' says Woolly Woolly Baa Lamb. 'That is better than all this talking.' He lifts his cold blue eyes and looks at each of us. 'We will rescue them tonight!' says he. 'Tonight!'

We nod our heads one after another. 'It is agreed,' we all mutter in our different voices.

'Hooray!' bleats Woolly up into the sky. He tramples his front hooves upon the grass.

Cow nods slowly. But her face is crumpled and worried. 'Tonight?' she whispers. 'So soon. I will help, of course I will. But where can we take the pups? Where will they be safe?'

I have no answer to that.

'I must go to the barn at once,' says I, 'and tell the pups.'

'I will come with you,' says Foxy Loxy whisking her wide and bushy tail. 'Now!' says she. Off she trots in her sliding foxy way. I bound after her.

Soon we are at the barn. I show her the hole I used the first time. 'This way leads to the pups,' says I. Without a word she slips through into the dark barn beyond. I scurry after her. When I get through I see that she is staring at the straw wall and the gap where the mesh hangs.

'Where are the pups?' says she. 'Are they in there?'

They are there. And they have seen us. It is Little Dog Nip who sees us first. His bright eyes find us out even in that gloom.

'Hyip! Hyip! I see strangers,' he cries out. Then 'Ratty! It is you,' he yelps, 'and someone else.'

He has seen Foxy Loxy.

He goes stiff from his paws to his tail end. His sharp nose trembles as he drinks in air to smell her better. His eyes go dark.

'Wild thing! Wild thing!' he hisses. 'I smell wild thing!'

He throws back his head to howl a warning. But

then thinks better of it. 'Perhaps she is your friend Ratty,' says he.

'She is a friend indeed,' says I. 'She has come to help to set you free. To let you out of here.'

'Oh yes?' says he. 'How can that be?'

'This is not a good place, Nip,' says I. 'You should get out and be free and find a better home.'

Nip listens with his pointed ears. 'You are going to help us get out?' says he at last. 'Are you sure it's all right, Ratty?'

'Yes, it is a good plan,' says I. I have my ratty paws crossed you can imagine. It is not a plan at all. Not a real plan. But we will get the pups out, that we can do. And after that we must hope for the best.

Nip stares at me. It is as if he sees what is in my

mind. He is only a little dog and not so old. But he is not stupid neither. 'Ummm,' says Little Dog Nip.

'You should go and tell the other pups,' says Foxy Loxy.

Nip turns and trots off. We see him push his nose at one pup, then another, then another. The pups get up. They listen. They jump and bark and run in circles. Then they go to tell their friends.

Foxy Loxy leaps up onto the high bale tops. She sits there with her bushy tail wrapped around her paws. I scramble up beside her.

'This is all so odd,' says Foxy Loxy. 'Some of the pups are just babies. But the pup in charge is older.'

'In charge?' says I. 'Oh no, he is not in charge. That is Little Dog Nip. I think he is a bit older. But he is just a pup like all the rest, no different from the rest.'

'Mmmm,' says Foxy Loxy. She blinks her amber eyes and pulls her tail closer about her.

The pups are yapping now and running in circles. 'A trip! A trip!' they squeak. 'We will see the Great Outside. We will be just like big doggos and see the World!'

'So many,' says Foxy Loxy. Her red brow furrows in a frown. 'It will be a hard journey. They are so small.'

I stare down at the pups. She is right but what else can we do?

'We need to be ready for tonight,' says I. 'I need to rest. I will find a place here.'

'You are not in your friendly city now,' says Foxy. 'Find a safe spot, rat friend. Hide away. Be careful.'

She is right, of course she is. Who knows better than she the way a ratty may be snapped up as he dozes? I slide down the straw bales and call out to Nip. 'We will come back as dark falls! Be ready.'

Foxy Loxy sweeps off across the dark floor and disappears out through the low gap. I bound off into the gloom of the barn and look for somewhere safe. I find a dark and dusty space under a tractor seat and curl up tight.

The last thing I see is Spider spreading her web above my head. Then I sleep.

It is a comfy spot and quiet. As I dream I hear the bleating of the sheep outside and once or twice the roar of a train. 'Just as Pup said,' I mutter to myself and doze again.

Jeth and Tone come back of course, but they do not disturb me in my dark corner. They make a noise and mutter and crash pails and whistle but what is that to me?

At last they go. The van drives off. And night comes.

Here comes Foxy Loxy through the hole.

'Ratty!' she calls. I am down from my safe place in a moment.

'It is now!' she says. 'The time is now. Let us rescue the pups!'

Rescue the pups! It sounds so simple. But it is not. First we have to pull down the mesh to make a way out. Foxy does that, scrabbling with her strong front paws. That is hard enough.

But when the pups come trotting out on their unsteady paws it gets much harder. Fifty pups have fifty minds and never two the same. We try to get them all together. We try to line them up.

'This way,' I squeak.

'This way,' yelps Nip.

The puppies turn and wave their heads this way and that. 'Where? How? Who?' they yap.

It is a long task but we do it at last. All the pups are here together. All facing one way. All ready.

'Now follow me,' I say to the pups. 'I will go through the hole first and Nip will help you follow.'

'I will come last of all,' says Foxy Loxy.

She is not easy in her mind. I see it. She flattens her ears back upon her neck. Her tail twitches to and fro. Her golden eyes flash this way and that.

'Oh Ratty,' she whispers, 'this does not feel safe. It cannot be safe.'

But we are here and we must carry on.

Off we go across the wide barn floor. Nip steps up to the hole. He turns to check the pups. 'All here?' he says. 'Let's go! Follow Ratty!'

I trot forward to take my place at the front. Just as I run towards the hole, a strange noise rises in the dark outside. A bleating. A mooing. A loud cry. 'Danger! Danger! The men are waiting for you! Go back! Danger!'

Woolly and Cow and all the sheep are shouting out a warning.

'I knew it!' says Foxy Loxy.

Her fur stands stiff upon her back. Her tail arches and bushes out. Her eyes are not like eyes at all but glowing pits of terror.

She is the last thing I see as I rush out through the gap to escape.

'What is happening?' I hear her hiss as I take my first leap and my last. I could tell her – if I was not trapped and caught and wrapped in sacking and a lost ratty.

I could tell her. Jeth and Tone are here, that is what! Outside the barn. Crouching in the dark.

They are waiting for us. They have big sacks with them. They hold a sack open to the gap in the wall. Into that sack I run. And after me all the pups, one by one.

When one sack is full, Jeth grabs another.

I know because I am in the first sack. It is seized and knotted shut and thrown aside. But still I hear the puppy feet, the little gasps, the thud of puppy bodies.

The puppies all around me in the sack whimper and cry out. But I have no tears for them. They will live. But what of Foxy Loxy?

'Oh Foxy!' I sob into my ratty fur. 'Oh wild friend, I have led you into danger. Mortal danger. They will not spare you.'

'Haha!' says Jeth. I hear him tying up the last sack. 'That is all the pups I think. Now for the fox! Tone my lad,' says he, 'this is a real fox hunt! None of that silly red coat stuff. There'll be a new fur rug for my cottage I think and an end to a wicked wild thing that tried to do us down!'

And here she comes. Now at last. Foxy Loxy. Their wild foe.

I cannot see her but I hear the rush of her fur against the metal. I hear the scrabble of hard paws. I hear the snick snack snick of sharp teeth. I hear the hiss in Foxy's throat as she fights for her life.

'Got her!' shouts Tone. Then 'Aaah!' his voice soars high with fright. 'Jeth – she's bitten me!'

Snack! The jaws close again.

'Oooh!' roars Jeth. 'She's got my thumb! The wicked thing! To the bone too. She is a savage beast she is. I'll get her!'

There is a heavy thud of fist on fur. I hear Foxy gasp. Then bite again.

The men roar both together. There is a spatter of drops onto the sacking over my head. It smells of blood. It is not fox blood.

'Blood!' cries Tone. 'I am bleeding bad,' he says. 'Real bad!'

'Me too!' shouts Jeth.

Then for a second there is silence.

Foxy Loxy is free. I know it.

I know the moment when she leaps from their hands. I hear the very second she jumps free into that cool night air.

The scamper of her paws dies into the dark.

'We lost her!' growls Jeth.

'But we have got that little rattykin!' says Tone. 'What a bad and cunning creature that is to be sure.'

'True,' says Jeth, 'and he will pay for this. But we must get to a doctor, you and me both. There is a lot of blood. And bites is bad, I know that.'

'We must pop the pups back,' says Tone. 'An extra bale will keep them safe. Without their friends they will go nowhere.'

The sacks are lifted up. Bounce, bounce, we go back into the barn.

The sacks are opened. The pups are poured out into the thick straw. But not I. Oh no. Jeth is waiting for me.

'Got you!' he snarls. He seals the sack again as my nose quivers out into the air. 'You have caused too much trouble. Just you wait,' says he.

The pups are frightened. I hear their puppy voices sad and low. 'It is best here,' they whisper. 'Outside is not nice. Outside is not safe.'

'That rat will gnaw his way out of the sack in no time,' says Tone. Tone is not so stupid as I thought he was.

'True,' says Jeth. 'Into the corn chest with him! That should settle his hash!' He laughs a great loud laugh.

I am whisked up into the air. I hear a heavy lid pushed up. Through the air I go and thud upon a hard wooden floor. The lid thumps down above me.

'Now for that doctor!' says Jeth and off they clump.

They go and I am left alone. I lie in the dark sack in the dark chest in the dark barn and I tremble.

CHAPTER 7

I lie in the dark all by my single self and I tremble.

But not for long. Ratties are ratties you know. We are not sit-about-and-cry sort of folk. I do not like the sack. But what are teeth for I ask you? Before Tone and Jeth are in their van, I have gnawed my way out of my sack.

Where does that get me?

Absolutely nowhere. That's where.

I am still in the corn chest. There is no chance, no chance at all, of getting out of it. The chest is old and solid and the lid fits like a snail's shell.

I can see nothing but black night. But there is fresh air from somewhere. With my long nose I find a circle of tiny holes, no wider than my claw's points, at each end of the chest. I cannot get out of the holes, of course I cannot. But they have kept the corn fresh. I can say so. I have eaten it.

Jeth did not mean to treat me kind but he did. This chest is half full of sweet dry corn. I can't eat it all. But I try my best.

I eat all night long. When the morning light comes poking through the holes, I am lying against one wall of the chest. My belly is round and stretched and full as it can be. My eyes are shut.

I am too full to worry. I will worry later.

Then I hear something.

A scream. It is a scream. From far away but loud, so loud. It pours through the silent barn air. It slams through the thick wood of my prison into my round ears.

I am on my feet now. And in a second I know what it is. It is Horse, White Horse. I have never heard a horse scream but it is her. There is no other creature strong enough to send this shout into the air.

But why? What is happening?

A second scream comes louder than the first. I hear a tramping thud of hooves on grass. White Horse is running and leaping. And she is screaming as she goes.

I stand in my wooden prison. I clutch my little ratty paws together. What is happening? Through the chest walls I hear Jeth and Tone. Far off. Outside the barn.

'What in blazes is going on?' yells Jeth.

'The horse is mad!' squeaks Tone. 'She has gone mad!

'You are right. She is crazy! Look at that!' – there is a

crash of wood breaking. 'Watch out there, Tone. Those feet will have you if you don't watch out!'

'What can we do?' cries Tone.

'We've got to catch her. Get her inside the barn. That's what.'

'Catch her! How?'

'I don't know, but we must!' shouts Jeth. 'It only takes one train to go past and there'll be some busy-body on the phone. It'll be vets and police and all the riffraff in no time. Then where will we be? We have to catch her.'

Tone says nothing. White Horse has feet like stone hammers and teeth like axes. I would not go close to her if she screamed at me.

The screaming goes on. 'Dear Horse,' I whisper. 'Be calm. Take care.' But I am talking to my own brown paws and no one hears me.

I hear the field gate crash open. And then silence.

Silence. Until at last there is the metal clink of the lock and the little door creaks open.

'Can we get her through here?' asks Tone. 'It is not so wide.'

'Have to,' says Jeth. 'At least she's quiet now. Like a lamb. I don't understand it. Don't understand it at all.'

'Come on girl,' says Tone. 'Easy does it!' His voice is shaking.

I hear the plod, plod, plod of heavy hooves upon the barn floor. Each step comes nearer to me in my dark chest.

'We'll put her in this corner,' says Jeth.

'What about a vet?' asks Tone. 'She was loopy mad out there. A danger to life and limb,' says Tone.

'A vet!' snorts Jeth. 'You are loopy mad yourself to think of it. What would the vet think of our little business? No indeed,' says Jeth.

They get White Horse a bucket of water. I hear them. She has frightened them good and proper. That is what I think.

At last they go. The door creaks, the chain clangs, the lock is turned. The van starts up and bounces off along the track.

'Ratty,' says Horse, so close that my ears tingle. 'Dear Ratty, where are you? I am here to get you out.'

I squeal. Then I close my eyes and almost I cry. 'White Horse,' says I, 'I must be close to you. I hear you so loud. I am in a thick dark box.'

'Aha,' says she, 'there is only one of those and it is here by my nose.'

I hear her soft breath whiffle through the tiny air holes in the box ends. 'In here?' she asks.

'Yes,' I squeak again. 'In here and wanting to be out of here.'

'Yes,' says she. 'Mmmm.'

There is a pause.

'It is not easy, Ratty friend,' says she. 'I wish it were.'

My heart sinks. If Horse, strong Horse, cannot do it I am a lost ratty indeed.

'You see,' says she, 'the chest is old and strong with

four thick legs to keep it off the ground. The lid is fastened tight as tight.' She leans her nose down. She talks straight through the little holes to me in my dark prison.

'There is only one thing I can do, Ratty,' says she. 'I must kick the box into a heap of little pieces. I have four new metal horseshoes on my feet. They will smash it up and no mistake. But, dear Ratty, you are inside the box.'

I understand in a moment. She will smash the box with her hard feet. I am in the box. She may smash me too. How can she not?

'Say yes or no, friend Ratty,' says she. 'It is risky. I can stand here and talk to you and hope for the best. Or I can smash your prison chest and hope that you are breathing still when it is broken up.'

Well that is clear enough.

'Smash on,' I say. My voice shakes, a little, as it must. 'Smash on, and I will try to keep my fur whole until the box breaks.'

I scuttle over to one of the corners. If her great feet crash up or sideways, the corner is my best chance. I lean back against the heavy wood.

Then it begins.

It is like thunder. It is like falling trees, and hammers. It is like the world ending. Most of all it is like the end of Ratty.

Horse's hooves whistle through the air – I hear them. I grab my ears and pull them flat against my

furry head. I lean back as far as I can go.

Smash! Her two back feet hit the bottom of the chest. Every grain of wood leaps and shakes. And so do I.

Smash again!

This time she hits the side wall. I am thrown down upon the floor. I open my mouth to squeal but there is no time for squealing. The feet are coming again. I leap back into my corner. Just in time.

Smash! I am hurled up and sideways like a floppy boneless thing.

But now I hear a crack! A splintering tearing crack!

The wooden floor splits open in two long jagged tears.

I tumble. I fall. Out through the air and down.

I know nothing more. Until later. Much later. I come back from far away. My head rests upon hard cool ground. I lift my round ears. All I hear is quiet and the sound of soft breathing. I open one eye.

White Horse is looking down at me. Her long face is sad. There are tears rolling down her bony nose. 'Oh Ratty,' says she, 'I thought you had Gone Away.'

'So did I,' says I. I roll over slowly. I try to stand. Stiffly.

'Dear friend,' says I. 'I am alive and you have saved me.'

'Can you move, Ratty?' asks Horse. 'It would be best to hide, you know. Those men will come back. They said so.'

I gaze up at her. 'You are right, White Horse,' says I. 'I shall do as you say. You are a true and wise friend. You do not look like a mad horse to me!'

Horse lifts her head and laughs a long whinny into the air. 'That was a good plan, was it not?' says she. 'They were frightened you know. It got me in here double quick – I knew it would.'

I nod my head. 'It was a brave and clever plan,' says I, 'and saved my ratty fur. Now I will hide.'

I try to scamper off. It is not easy. I limp and lurch but off I go. I find the same dark shelter on the silent tractor. I curl up under Spider's web once more.

I sleep.

It is late in the day when the men return. They

come in quietly and peer round the little door. I watch from my dark corner.

'The horse is quiet now,' whispers Tone.

'You can take her out into the field if she is quiet,' says Jeth. 'Then we can have fun with that Ratty – the little perisher will pay!'

They clump up the barn to where White Horse stands, still and silent.

Tone gasps. He puts his hand up to his mouth.

'Oh Jeth,' says he. 'She has been loopy mad again. She has smashed the chest!' He stares at Horse. He is shaking.

Jeth whistles softly through his teeth.

'She is a wild horse this one,' says he. 'We will sell her quick. But what about the rattyo? Where is he?'

'Well,' says Tone, 'he must be dead and gone and squashed I think. I cannot see him. The bottom of the box is all in pieces. And so is he I do believe.'

'Tut tut,' says Jeth. 'I would have liked to finish him myself but one rat gone is good news, no matter how. As for that fox, it is the Hunt tomorrow,' says he, 'perhaps they will catch her. Then our troubles will be over. We can make our money and be as happy as we should be, Tone my friend.'

Tone smiles all over his face.

'Get the horse some food, Tone,' says Jeth. 'Then we can feed the pups. They go tomorrow,' says he, 'but it is not what I planned. All this trouble at once! Nothing goes right.'

Tone gets a sack and pours some horse food into a bucket. Horse whiffles her soft nose over her food. She picks at it with her soft mouth and scoffs it down. She is content.

Jeth steps over into the puppy pen. I hear the puppies yelp and gobble up their food.

Now the two men turn towards the far end of the barn. Where are they going?

I watch them from my safe corner. I watch them hard.

'We'd better feed the other lot too,' says Jeth. 'They do not take much after all.'

'I hate the smell of them,' says Tone. 'What horrid dirty doggos they are!'

They step past the tractor and over to a low door. Then they step through and vanish from sight.

A smell floats down the barn.

What is that smell? There must be another room, another space, beyond that barn wall. Who lives there? I stare but there is nothing I can see from here.

At last the men come back. They slam the door behind them. 'All done for today,' says Jeth. 'I will get that horse sold quick as quick. Grab her rope will you, Tone, and we'll get her outside again. Let us hope that she stays quiet.'

Tone looks worried but he goes over to White Horse. He loops a rope around her neck and leads her down the barn. Horse steps forward peaceful as can be. Tone is happy at this.

'Perhaps she will be better now,' says Tone.

'I do not care,' growls Jeth. 'We must sell her as soon as maybe. Like the pups. They go tomorrow. What a mess! This is not what I planned.' He trudges off down the barn. He opens the little door. Tone steps through leading White Horse. The door shuts. I hear her hooves clip clop across into the field.

They have gone and I am safe. And I am almost as good as new. I stretch my short legs. I bend my back. I wave my round ears. All's well with me.

But now I have a new question to answer.

Who else is shut in this cold barn? Who needs feeding beyond that dark wall?

I must find out.

CHAPTER 8

I must find out who lives in the barn end.

I scuttle out of the barn and into the bright sunshine. Then I turn and scamper along the rusted metal walls to the far end of the barn.

I stop and I listen with my big ears. Nothing. All is silence.

I sniff with my long nose. That is better. My nose tells me that this is the place. The smell in my nose is the same smell. And what a smell it is.

Now ratties are not fancy folk you know well. We do not like clean floors and swept corners. But there are good smells and bad smells.

Good smells come when things die and rot and ratties eat them. That is one smell.

But this is the smell of sad things who are not cared for. We ratties like our coats to shine and gleam. We like clean paws and smart whiskers. This smell is of creatures who cannot get clean, who stand in their own muck. Even Pig hates that.

And these creatures are not pigs. Oh no. My long nose tells me that. Behind this barn wall are doggos, more doggos.

There is a crack in the high barn side. I push through. I look about me.

This end of the barn is like a separate shed. Small and narrow and high.

In the grey dim light I see a line of short posts. From each post hangs a chain. At each chain end there lies a doggo, a grown-up doggo.

Even from here I see their dull eyes, their hollow sides. They lie on stained straw. They are still as statues and silent as stones.

I crawl towards the silent shapes. I am a careful

ratty. These are doggos, teeth and all. I crawl forward in the straw. I stop just where I think the chains will stretch.

I rise up on my short legs and stare. Here they are. Eight doggos, eight mother doggos. So this is where the mother doggos are! But why?

Their eyes are blank and empty. Their ears do not turn and listen like any doggo ears that I have known. Their noses do not sniff the air like doggo noses should.

They are a sad sad sight to see. Doggos are not my favourites, they are not. But these make even my ratty heart weep.

'Friends,' I say. 'I am Ratty. Why are you here? I do not understand.'

Two or three stir but none replies.

'A doggo can never be a ratty's best pal,' says I, 'but no doggo should be like this!'

A brown dog lifts her head and stares at me. White hairs spot her muzzle. She is weak but her eyes are angry. 'We are not doggos,' she says, 'we are machines.'

'Machines!' I squeak.

It is not true. A living doggo smell fills the air around them.

'Not machines,' I whisper. 'No, no, it cannot be.'

'Puppy machines,' says a pale dog in the corner. 'That is what my friend means. This is a puppy factory. And we are the puppy machines.'

I stare. My breath is almost stopped. What does she mean? How can a living breathing doggo be a machine? It makes no sense.

'Machines is what we are,' says Brown Doggo. 'That is what the men think. We have pups after pups, time after time. Each puppy family that we have, the pups are smaller, weaker. When we get too tired and the pups too small, we will Go Away. That will be that.'

I am turned to stone. Like them I sit cold and still. Like them my breath can scarce move in my throat.

'Oh friends,' I say at last. 'How can we help you? What can we do?'

'Who is this we?' says Brown Doggo. 'And who are you?'

'I am Ratty, from the far city,' says I, 'come to help you.'

'But who,' she says again 'is we? I see only one of you.'

'Oh I am not alone,' says I, 'I have friends. Strong, brave friends. They will rescue you.'

'Where are your friends? Who are they?'

'They are Cow, and Woolly Woolly Baa Lamb. They are in the field outside and they are heroes.'

'Aha,' she yelps with laughter. Grim laughter. 'You cannot fool us. Cows are not heroes. Nor sheep neither.'

I think for a moment. 'Well,' says I, 'I suppose it is true that most cows, and most sheep too, like a quiet life and harmony. But my friends are different. They are heroes indeed,' says I, 'and they will rescue you.'

A spotted doggo in the corner lifts her pointed muzzle. 'Only people can help us,' says she. 'That is the truth. We need people to unlock these chains. And people to stop the men who hurt us. But you can help the pups. Get the pups out if you can.'

'Yes, yes,' says Brown Doggo, 'do that and we will be happy.'

'We have tried,' says I sadly. 'We failed. But we will try again.' Then I frown. 'But why are you worried about the pups? They look quite well you know, and fat.'

'Of course they do,' say all the doggos with one breath. 'That is the plan. The men take them away from us. They feed them to make them fat but it is not good food. Then they sell them. But our pups are not strong pups. How can we have strong pups? They need special care and love and kindness. And what they get is none of that. Help our pups,' say the voices from the grey dark.

I put my paws up to my furry head. There is too much to think about. I cannot think alone. I need my friends.

'I will go,' says I, 'but I will come back. Trust me.'

I trot slowly over to the barn wall. I creep through into the bright sunshine. I sit there for a long time. My head is full of sadness.

This is worse than I had thought.

I am so sad I do not hear the click of doggo claws

upon the hard earth. A shadow falls across me. I look up and here is Nip, Little Dog Nip. He is out in the bright sun, all on his ownyo.

'Nip friend,' I squeak. 'You are out of the barn and free!'

'Yes yes,' yaps he. 'We were shut up tight at first you know, but now it is back to normal. But you are alive and breathing Ratty friend. That is good news. I heard that you were dead and gone.'

'That is what the bad men think,' says I. 'But that is all the good news that I know. There is more bad news than my ratty heart can bear. That is the truth.'

Nip wags his little tail but he is puzzled. 'What can you mean, Ratty?' says he. 'All is well. The little pups were frightened of the sacks and all the shouting. But they are happy now. So what can make you sad?'

I turn my eyes and stare at him. 'Nip – how did the men know about the rescue?' I ask. 'Some pup told them, that is sure enough. Who told them, Nip?'

Nip stares back at me. He is silent for a long moment.

'You mean there is a pup who tells the men?' he says at last.

'Yes,' says I. 'A bad pup who is on their side. Who could it be?'

Nip looks at me in a sad sort of way. 'Bad is a hard word,' says he.

'It is a hard word,' says I. 'But it is the true word. Those two men knew our plan. They were waiting. And they almost killed Foxy Loxy. That is what they meant to do.'

'I know,' says he, 'but Ratty, what should a pup do? If a pup feels that Jeth is his person, or Tone perhaps. If a pup feels that,' says Nip, 'he might have to tell. You know that. It is a good doggo who is loyal to his person.'

I shake my head. 'I suppose so,' says I. 'But it is strange for me. I do not know who I can trust.'

'What do you mean?' says Nip.

'I am not used to this,' says I. 'My friends are my friends. I trust them. They trust me. It is all clear like bright day. But nothing is clear in this dark place.'

Nip shakes his small head and sighs a small sigh. 'It is a dark place,' says he. 'That is the truth.'

I stand up on my four paws. 'I will go now,' I say. 'All

you pups must be free, and soon. We shall succeed no matter who betrays us.'

'No matter who,' says Nip.

'I must find my friends,' says I.

Off I scamper. I leave him staring after me.

I scuttle under the field fence. I trot slowly over the green grass. I see White Horse over by the fence. Woolly is close by, and Cow. They are eating, of course they are. They are herbivores as you know well.

'I wish I could eat green grass and not think sad thoughts,' I whisper to myself. Cow has heard me. She flaps her big black ears towards me.

Her face lights up. 'Oh Ratty friend,' she cries. 'It is such joy to see you. We were so worried until Horse worked out how she could rescue you. But Ratty, your face is sad, so sad. And there is a funny smell on your fur. What has happened?'

Woolly stares and sniffs the air and stares again. 'Something is wrong,' says he. 'Something bad. Something worse. Tell us at once and we will bear it.'

White Horse leans her long neck down to sniff me. 'Tell,' she says.

I stare up at their big kind faces. Then I sit back upon the sunny grass and tell them what I know.

'Dear friends,' says I. 'I have a sad sad story to tell you. I have found out what the bad men are doing. The pups are just one bit of it. Their mothers are in the barn too. They are as thin as bones. They know that their puppies are not strong but the bad men sell the pups as soon as they are big enough.' I feel tears rising in my hard ratty eyes.

'Oh Ratty,' says Cow. 'We must help the mother doggos. We must.'

'Well,' says Woolly, 'we might. But when we tried to help the pups, it all went wrong. Why did it go wrong, Ratty?'

'That is another bad thing,' says I. 'I am sure that some pup told Jeth and Tone what we had planned. There is a bad pup there somewhere. I have just been talking to Nip about it.'

'You were talking to Nip were you?' says Cow sadly.

'Nip,' says White Horse in the same sad way.

I look up and stare into their faces. 'Why not?' says I. 'What do you mean?'

Cow looks at Horse and Horse looks at Cow. At last Cow speaks. 'It might be Nip you know,' says she. 'Did you think of that?'

'Oh no!' I cry. 'Not Nip. He is a brave smart doggo and he is my friend.'

'But Ratty dear,' says White Horse, 'perhaps he is Jeth's friend too or Tone's. A doggo is a doggo you know. They stick by their people, doggos do. They think it is right.'

Woolly snorts through his hard white nose. 'Any pup that tells our plans to those bad men is a bad doggo. That is what I say.' He stamps his feet and looks very fierce indeed.

I sit and say nothing. My heart is sadder than it was

before. 'Oh Cow. Oh Horse,' says I, 'I hope that you are wrong. If Nip has chosen Jeth or Tone for his friend he will have a sad life. They are bad bad people and not kind to animals, that we know.'

Woolly is thinking his own thoughts. 'We can trust no one but our four selves,' says he.

'And Foxy Loxy too of course,' says I.

Just then I see her. A red shadow flitting between the grey sheep shapes. It is Foxy Loxy, here with us again. She looks weary. Her fur is matted on one side.

'Oh Foxy!' we all cry. 'You are safe! And free!'

She sees us staring at her stained fur. 'That mark is Jeth's doing,' says she, 'but I left a sharper mark on him. On both of them!' She bares her pointed teeth and smiles a fierce and foxy smile.

'Dear Foxy,' says I, 'we have been having a sad talk. Whatever we plan, we cannot tell the pups. One of them told the men about the escape. They must have!'

'A pup betrayed our plan!' says she. 'Well that is doggos all over. They put their person first, every time. Even when that person is bad as can be.'

I sigh and think of Nip's bright face. I hope it is not he who told the men. 'There is worse news,' I say. Then I tell her about the mother doggos.

Foxy Loxy snarls back her russet lip until I see each one of her sharp white teeth. 'They are bad bad men!' she hisses. 'We must beat them!'

Woolly stamps his feet and blows through his white nose. 'We must beat them!' he bleats. 'I think it is time for us big ones to try. We need hard heads and heavy shoulders and iron hooves. It is sheep time, and cow time, and horse time. Leave this to us, Ratty!'

I stare and then I droop. My friends do not want me. I pull my tail around me and huddle to the ground.

'Oh Ratty dear,' says Cow, 'it is not good to be left out. I know it. But you are not left out. You have done so much. But perhaps now is the time for us big ones, who are not so clever.'

I look up at her smiling face. And then at Woolly, worried now, and kindly Horse. 'Of course we need you still, Ratty,' says Woolly, 'but sheep do not often get the chance for big adventures.' He stands tall on his woolly legs. His eyes sparkle like blue stars. 'Our sheep adventure come at last!' he cries. 'Our woolly glory!'

'And I shall help too,' says Horse, 'with my hard feet.'

Foxy Loxy is thinking her own thoughts. 'What about the mother doggos?' says she.

'They are the saddest of all,' says Cow. Woolly shakes his head. White Horse stares glumly at her two front feet.

'I do not see how we can help them,' says I. 'They need people to unlock their chains. Even you big things cannot do that. And where are people in this country place?'

'It is the Hunt tomorrow,' says Foxy Loxy very quiet. 'There are lots of people in the Hunt.'

'The Hunt!' says White Horse. She lifts her head in

an excited sort of way. 'That always looks such fun to me, all that running and jumping and chasing!'

Foxy Loxy's eyes go chill. 'It is fun for some,' says she, and wraps her tail close about her.

I am still thinking. 'I do not see how we can help the mother doggos,' I say.

'Mmmm,' says Cow. I see in her eyes the glinty gleamy look that I saw at the City Farm.

'Mmmm,' says Foxy Loxy. She lifts her sharp nose and sniffs the air. Then she rises to her four paws and shakes herself. 'I have work to do,' says she. 'Perhaps I will see you tomorrow.'

She is gone. Before we can say a word. Gone into the dark.

Woolly snorts. 'I thought she would help us,' says he. 'Wild things! You cannot trust them.'

Then he turns to me. 'We big things have to make our plan, Ratty. We will meet you in the morning.'

So Cow and Horse and he trot off into the dusk. They stand against the railway fence with their three big heads together. They begin to talk.

I am alone as ratties can be. And tired too. So I go to my tree root. I hide deep in its hollows and curl up tight. Tomorrow is tomorrow is tomorrow. It can look after itself. Now is sleep time.

I sleep as tranquil as if I was in my own farm bed with all the city about me. Dawn breaks. I open my eyes and I am a fresh and frisky ratty ready for anything.

'Today is it,' I whisper to myself. 'Today is the great day. Today is now!'

I stretch and yawn and bare my yellow teeth. Then off I bound through the wet morning grass to find my friends.

CHAPTER 9

I bound along in the bright morning air to find my friends. I pick my way between the sheep, and then I stop. Something is different! Something has changed. I look this way and that. I puzzle. What is different?

Then I know.

There are more sheep.

Lots more. The field is packed with sheep. I look harder. Some of them are strangers. They do not have blue circles on their backs. They have stars, and crosses, and letters or nothing at all. These are stranger sheep! They are friendly and nod their heads at me but strangers they are.

I do not know what to think. I scurry on until I find White Horse.

'Oh White Horse!' I cry. 'Have you noticed? There are lots of new sheep here. The field is full of them. Where can they have come from? And when?'

Horse smiles her soft smile.

'They came at night,' says she. 'They came along the railway bank. They have travelled from far and near. Last night Woolly bleated to his sheep friends in the field next door. Those sheep passed on the message and so it went, field after field, to far-off places that we do not know. Sheep have been coming in since mid-night. Jump up and see,' says she.

I grab her long mane and scramble up onto her high shoulder. I stare. Our field is full of grey round backs.

I look further, beyond the barn. I gasp. All the other fields are full too. They are white with sheep, grey with sheep. From here to the far line where the sky ends.

'Oh White Horse,' I whisper, 'I did not know. What is a ratty compared to this?'

'A ratty is very important,' says Horse, 'but just you wait and see. Things will happen now!'

I do not have to wait long. Rrrum. Thump. Bump. Along the lane comes the tractor. And on the top I see Jeth and Tone. They are chatting away. They have not seen. And then they do. The tractor stops. Slam. Bang.

'Oh Tone,' says Jeth, 'I am dreaming. I am dreaming sheep. Do you see what I see?'

'Jeth!' squeaks Tone. 'I see sheep as far as my eye will go. What is happening?'

Down they both leap onto the hard ground. They scratch their heads. They blink and stare. Then Jeth gets a cunning look on his face.

'These are extra sheep,' says he, 'new sheep. We

could sell them for ourselves and Farmer would never know.'

'Yes, yes,' says Tone. 'Let us go and take a look. There are hundreds. We must count them!'

Both together they step forward to the fence. Both together they reach the big field gate. Both together they open it.

And that is that. Every sheep is waiting for the gate to open. Every sheep leaps forward.

Bang. One hard curly head hits Jeth. Thump. Another hits Tone. Down they go. Thud thud go the woolly sheep bodies between the gateposts. Click clack go the pointed hooves. Over Jeth and Tone.

But they are strong men and fierce men too. For a second they lie there like doormats. Then they are up. Jeth rolls one way and Tone rolls the other. They spring to their feet. They stand by the fence gasping. They are covered in little pointed marks of sheep feet. They are not happy.

'I will murder all of them,' yells Jeth. 'No woolly thing knocks me over!'

'But what can we do?' squeaks Tone.

The sheep are pouring out like a grey and woolly river. They pack through the gate. They fill the track.

They crowd towards the high barn.

'Get to the tractor!' shouts Jeth. 'We will squash them all. Then we will go and raise the alarm. We'll stop them!'

But the sheep have heard him. From all sides sheep leap up onto the tractor. They lie over its seat, over its wheels, a woolly blanket over all that metal machine.

Jeth and Tone stare and blink. 'It is creepy,' mutters Jeth. 'You would think they understand what we say.'

Tone's eyes are popping. 'I do not like this Jeth,' he whispers. 'They frighten me!'

'Now you know what it feels like,' mutters Woolly Woolly Baa Lamb. He trots past White Horse and me. His face is bright and fierce. He is an action lamb. A

hero lamb. And this is his glory time.

He pushes forward into the space in front of the high barn doors. 'Friends,' he bleats, 'you know why you are here. This barn is a sad bad place. It has stood too long. We will knock it down!'

All the sheep shout out together, 'We will knock it down!' They bleat so loud that I bury my ears in Horse's mane. It is like a clap of thunder in a summer sky.

'We have a friend to strike the first blow,' cries Woolly Woolly Baa Lamb. 'A friend even stronger than we are. Dear Horse,' says he.

Well this is news to me. And here I am on Horse's high back. I cling on tight as tight and wish that I was somewhere else.

Horse wastes no time. Clip clop she trots forward. The sheep make way for her. She steps in front of the rusting barn doors.

Woolly blinks his pale eyes. Horse nods her head. I know what her hard feet can do so I twist my four paws into her mane. I cling to her neck as tight as my little ratty legs can cling. I close my eyes.

She pivots on her strong legs. Then down goes her head and CRASH! I hear her metal shoes hit metal doors. The first blow.

The long muscles in her neck and back move under my paws. She bunches her shoulders. Then down goes her head again, out go her long back legs, and CRASH! The second blow.

There is a cracking tearing sound. The doors are old and rusted. Every seam is weak with rust. They cannot last long.

Two more kicks. Then a great bleating starts up around us. The barn doors hang in strips of broken metal.

'Hooray for Horse! Hooray! Hooray!' bleat a thousand sheep voices. 'She has broken the doors. Now it is our turn.'

Horse turns and snorts with triumph. She rises on her back legs and waves her front hooves in the air. It is too much for me.

Up I go. Off I go. Into the air I fly like a furry ball. One squeal. Then down!

I am a bird with no wings and that is not a good thing to be.

Down. But not onto the hard ground. No. Down onto woolly softness. The sea of woolly backs catches me. I bounce. I slide. Then at last I slip to the ground, soft and easy and safe as can be.

Just in time.

Five big rams push forward into the front row. So big, so heavy they are, that each of them looks like two sheep inside one woolly skin. And in front of them is Woolly Woolly Baa Lamb.

He is not so big as they. But he is brave and nothing will stop him.

'Now!' cries Woolly.

'Now!' roar the rams.

'Now!' bleats every sheep from every field for miles around.

And now it is. Forward they run, forward they leap. All together. Crash go their heads. Thump go their shoulders. Trip trap trip go their hard forked feet.

And down goes the barn wall, doors and all.

The barn is open wide. The light pours in. The wind flutters the spiders' webs. The sun glitters down on the metal of the sleeping tractors.

And in the middle, clear to see, is the puppy pen. Fifty puppy faces peer out at us through the meshed gap. Fifty puppy bodies quiver with terror. In front of them stands Nip, Little Dog Nip. He is dazzled by the sun that streams in on him but he alone is brave. He bristles with rage.

'Whoever you are,' says he, 'you will not pass me. You will not take the pups. I will defend us all.' He bares his sharp and tiny teeth at us.

Then he sees me. He stares. He bristles. Then he seems to shrug his small shoulders.

'Ratty,' says he. 'Of course.'

'We are come to let you out,' I cry. 'You are a brave heart Nip, but you do not need to fight us!'

'I am too small,' says Nip, 'to fight so many, even I know that.' He laughs a doggo laugh. 'I am too young and too small. When I grow up perhaps it will be different.'

'No need for fighting now at any rate,' says I. 'Let us get these pups out into the sunshine.'

The pups are still frightened at all the noise. Their eyes pop to see the sheep. But I talk, and I explain, and Horse talks and explains and at last they understand. Out they come through the gaping wall of the barn into the sunlight.

Their eyes pop all over again when they see Jeth and Tone, still pressed up against the fence. They goggle more when they see the sheep on top of the tractor.

But soon, soon all the pups come together. Cow leads them off down the lane and Woolly trots beside her. The sheep follow close behind the pups and keep them all together. 'It is a new thing for sheep to herd doggos,' says Woolly.

Some of the pups stop almost at once. They sit

down and whine. They are too small to trot along a hard road. Kindly sheep are all around. Soon the pups are riding high on soft woollen backs.

'I will stay back here with White Horse,' I call out to Woolly. 'I will make sure all is well.'

Woolly is too busy to listen. He has come to the grey road at the end of the track. A car has stopped. A man jumps out. He stares and stares. 'Well goodness me,' cries the man. 'Sheep and more sheep and puppies too!' He lifts a phone to his ear and talks so fast we cannot understand him. Then another car appears. It screeches to a stop.

Woolly does not care. 'Watch out!' he bleats. 'We sheep are on our way.' He steps forward. The woolly river moves after him.

I wait on Horse's high back. I watch the sheep go past me. There are so many of them. The air is full of dust and bleating.

As the fields empty, Jeth and Tone begin to stir. 'We must get out of here,' says Jeth. 'Nothing but trouble will come of this. Time to go, Tone lad.'

'Too right,' says Tone.

They pick their way through the moving sheep. They walk past the tractor, still under its sheep cover. They set off along the track into the far fields. I watch their backs as they trudge away.

'Good riddance,' says Horse. She is a kindly horse but she does not look kind when she stares after Jeth and Tone. 'Bad men,' says she.

The sheep are almost past us now. Horse turns her head to trot after them down the lane. I gaze back at the ruined barn.

The barn looks empty now. The pups are all gone. But the mother doggos are there, I know they are. What can we do? I shake my head and ponder.

Then I look again. I see a movement.

One pup remains.

Round the corner of the barn comes Nip. He stares after me with his bright eyes. He gives a single wag of his fierce tail.

My heart sinks in my ratty chest. I understand. He cannot come with us. He is the friend of Jeth and Tone.

He sets back his pointed head. He opens his mouth and gives a last fierce yap into the air. Then he turns and trots away. He trots after Jeth and after Tone. He chose his masters long ago. He cannot change now.

'Oh Nip,' I whisper to myself, 'you were not our friend as I believed. You are a friend to bad men. Bad cruel men. What kind of life will you have?'

Horse starts to trot. The distance widens. 'I hope you may be happy, dear Nip,' I say, 'I hope you can be happy.'

As I bounce away on Horse's high back, the tears run down my ratty face.

White Horse has not seen what I have seen. She

trots on. After a while I sit up and wipe my tears away and look about me. The road is sloping uphill. Horse slows down to a walk. The sheep are right in front of us. They are trotting as if they mean to go a long way.

But who is this, pushing her way back through the sheep? Coming towards us?

Cow!

She is trotting back down the hill as fast as she can go. Her long forked feet go slip slip slip along the road. She is heading back towards the barn.

'Cow!' I squeak from my high perch. 'What are you doing?'

Cow stops for a moment. She is breathing hard. Cows are not made for running fast.

'The mother doggos! We cannot leave them, you know!' says she. 'The pups are safe. Woolly leads them and there are people there now. But we must get the mother doggos out too. Foxy Loxy had a plan but she would not tell me what it was. I must go back and see!'

She lifts her big front feet and starts to trot again. Away she goes.

I chew my long whiskers. What should I do?

I stand up tall upon Horse's high back. I stare back over the hedge to where the barn stands, ruined now. And as I look, I hear a sound.

Not a bleat.

Not a voice.

114

Not a puppy's whine.

No. It is a horn. A hunting horn.

'Oh Horse!' I cry. The high horn yelps again.

And then I see them.

Over the green fields – horses and dogs and people. Horses galloping, hounds running, red coats and black hats. It is the Hunt.

The Hunt! Pouring over hedge and ditch and broad green fields.

And close in front, flying for her life, is Foxy Loxy.

CHAPTER 10

Foxy Loxy is running for her life.

I stare. For one terrible moment I stare.

Then, 'Horse, White Horse,' I cry. 'Turn back. At once. Gallop as fast as ever you can. Foxy Loxy is in danger. Her life is lost if we cannot save her!'

Horse rears up upon her back legs but this time I do not tumble off. I cling to her mane. I swing as she turns. I lean forward as she crashes down. She thunders back along the hard road.

Past Cow we go. Cow cannot run so fast as Horse. Cows are not racy sorts of creatures. But she will come as quick as she can. White Horse thunders on. Back down the road. Back along the track. She skids to a stop in front of the ruined barn. Now she sees as well as I do.

Foxy Loxy is running through the field beside the railway bank. She stretches out as fast as she is able but she tires. She tires. Everyone sees that. Her tongue is lolling out. Her coat is matted with mud and briar. Her tail drags upon the ground.

Her running time is running out.

Where is she heading?

The hounds are close behind her now. In front of all is one great dog, mottled and tall. His heavy jaws pant to bite her. His legs drive on like metal pistons to carry him to victory.

'Seize her, Griper! Take her! Get her! Griper is there!' sings out the Huntsman.

But no. Something is wrong. Griper slides to a stop. He has lost his fox!

She has vanished.

I guess, but Griper does not. He lays his great nose to the ground and sniffs forward.

'She must be in the barn at the far end,' I whisper into Horse's ear. 'That is her plan!'

'She is a brave one,' says Horse. 'We must not fail her now.' Horse leaps forward into the barn. She gallops through it. At the far end she stops in front of the dark door.

Behind that door the mother doggos lie. Behind that door is Foxy Loxy.

Horse does not wait or pause. Up come her flashing metal feet. One blow. Then another.

The door springs wide. Horse steps forward. The room is dim but light enough to see. There in front of us are the posts. There are the chains and the still doggo shapes. And there, high on a straw bale, is Foxy Loxy. Her head is laid upon the straw. Her eyes are closed. Her sides heave and heave as if she will never have enough breath, ever again.

She is not safe. Griper has found the way. We see his broad black nose in the crack in the barn side.

'Here!' he howls, he sings out. 'Here, comrades. Our prey is here! Come here! The kill is ours!'

His broad paws start to scrabble at the ground. The whole pack is with him. They dig, they scratch. At last there is space enough. Here they come! The pack is through and with us!

Griper is first. He runs forward. He stops in the centre of that dim and smelling place. He gives the mother doggos just one look, no more. He is a hound and foxes are his prey.

'You are mine,' says he to Foxy Loxy on her bale of straw.

'Now, now!' howls the pack behind him.

'No no!' neighs Horse high and shrill.

'No no!' I squeak.

'Who will stop me?' says Griper. He leers around him. 'A horse? And a ratty, so small a ratty that I could gobble him up in half a breath? I do not think so.'

'I will stop you!' cries a voice from the doorway. Here is Cow, panting through her wide nose and trotting as fast as her feet will go. 'I will stop you!' She sweeps forward over the dirty straw. She turns and stands in front of Foxy Loxy where she lies on her

high bale. She lowers her sharp cow horns.

Griper is at a stand. He does not want to risk those fierce points. I would not either if I was him. Then just as he thinks what next, there is a rustle in the straw behind him.

The mother doggos are on their tired feet.

Brown Doggo growls from the darkness. 'No fox would run here to save herself. She came here to save us. It was for us!'

Foxy nods her tired head.

'For us!' calls another voice.

Then the mother doggos call out one and all, 'She has risked so much for us, we will not fail her! We will save her with our last strength. Great hound – fight us if you dare! Fight us all!'

Griper stares.

The mother doggos step out of the shadows. They are thin as winter hedges. They are so weak that they can hardly pull their chains across the straw. But they come. They step forward each and every one. They step forward and stand shoulder to shoulder. They lower their thin heads. They bare their white teeth. They wrinkle their grim foreheads.

They stand on either side of Cow where she waves her sharp and pointed horns. A doggo wall in front of Foxy's high resting place.

Griper stares and stares on. He cannot fight doggos and a cow. That is not his job.

Now White Horse steps forward. I lean down from

my high perch upon her shoulder.

'Wait a while, big doggo hound,' says I to Griper. 'There may be more to think of.'

Just then there is a thud of feet. Through the door steps Huntsman and a round lady with a pink face.

'Griper, fall back!' calls Huntsman in a voice that makes the barn ring. 'And all the rest of you, fall back! What is this? What is this?'

He stops. He stands still as a tree. He stares like Griper. 'What is this?' he whispers.

He is not looking at Foxy so quiet on her bale. Oh no. He is looking at the doggos. 'Oh bad, bad, bad,' says he. 'Who did this? These poor creatures. Whose work is this?' He lifts his head. He is getting angry. 'Who is to blame for this?' says he. His voice is loud now like his own hunting horn.

Behind him the pink-faced lady is staring too.

'How cruel!' she cries. 'How bad! This can't be Farmer's work.'

'No indeed,' says Huntsman. 'Farmer is good to his creatures, as much as he is able. This is someone else's doing. We will put a stop to this and now. Whoever did this, they will pay!'

But, thinks I, Jeth and Tone are far away. I do not think that paying is what they mean to do.

'There should be a law against keeping doggos in such a place,' snorts the pink faced lady.

'There is,' says Huntsman. 'We must let these crea-tures free and then find the bad folk. Someone in the

Hunt must have some pliers or a cutter. These chains are not so strong you know.' Out he tramps and Griper after him, then all the other hounds.

The pink faced lady stays and stares at the doggos. 'Oh doggos,' says she. 'You have had sad times. I see that. But no more. I shall take all of you to my own home. You will be healthy and happy and the finest doggos in all this country. I promise you that.'

In a trice Huntsman is back. He has a friend with him, a big man with a red face and big hands. 'It is these chains that are the problem,' says Huntsman. 'But you can fix them, I am sure.'

'You're right there,' says the man. He turns to the doggos where they stand. 'Trust us,' says he. 'You will be free. We love our doggos. This badness makes my blood boil over. How I wish I could meet up with the person who did this. They would be sorry then.'

He bends over the doggos, each in turn. He cuts each chain with a sharp metal thing he has in one hand. The chains fall to the ground. The doggos stand there free.

Brown Doggo lifts her battered head. 'Are we free?' she says in a voice so quiet I can hardly hear it. 'Is this freedom?'

Huntsman is almost crying. If he was not so tough I would think that there was water in his eyes. 'Please stay with them,' says he to the pink-faced lady. 'I will go and call the police. We will find the bad folk who have done this. And quick too!'

So the pink-faced lady stays. She sits on the straw. The mother doggos flop down beside her. She feeds them biscuits from her pocket. 'Not long now,' says she. 'A vet must look at you of course. All will be well. You will see.'

'Foxy, dear fox, clever bold Foxy Loxy,' I whisper from Horse's high shoulder. 'You have done it. You have won. They are safe. But are you safe, my friend?'

Foxy Loxy opens one amber eye and looks at me for just a moment. 'I am well enough,' says she. 'I will rest here awhile with my new friends. No one will hurt me, you will see. I shall rest.' She closes her eyes again and lays her head upon her paws.

She is right. No one hurts her. The hounds run in and out but they do not stir her way. The men come in and out, and ladies too. Then policemen and vets and other folk, so many that it seems the whole world is here.

'This is too much for me,' says I. It is too much for Foxy too. I see her leap softly down and slink out of the barn. She trots across to the railway bank and slides into the brambles, to where her warm den is hidden.

Horse and Cow and I step back along the barn into the light. More surprises. There is a helicopter over-head. I know that's what it is, because Horse tells me. She has seen one once before.

A man comes running past us with his camera. 'Have you seen the roads?' he shouts to someone in the barn. 'Sheep, wall to wall! No moving that way! Helicopters or horses, that's the only way to get about today!' He laughs and off he scrambles for more pictures.

'Well dear friends,' says I, 'I do believe that all is well here. Shall we find out how Woolly is faring? His sheep have caused a great stir with all these people. He will be pleased, I'm sure.'

'Let us go,' says Cow. White Horse turns after her along the track. It is empty now and quiet.

'I shall go gentle and slow,' says White Horse. 'I have had enough excitement for one day.' So we three have a quiet walk of it while helicopters buzz overhead and the first cars come through.

We find Woolly in a field. There are people in the field and cars and cameras. The pups are lying in a sleeping heap upon the ground while people watch over them. The sheep are catching up on eating time.

I slide down from Horse's high back and look about me.

'You missed the best bit,' says Woolly. 'A heli-flying-thing arrived. People jumped out and it was television they said. Just like Chee talked about. Perhaps they are the same people. Anyway they are bringing special vans to take the pups to somewhere safe. The Television Man says that every pup must have a good home now, and a safe place. He says they will need special homes because they are not strong you know.

That is what he says,' says Woolly Woolly Baa Lamb.

'I am glad of that,' says I. 'It is time someone was careful with those pups.'

'The Television Man says it was puppy farming,' says Woolly with a wrinkle on his curly forehead. 'Puppy farming!'

'I have not heard of that before,' says I. 'What does it mean?'

'It means that Jeth and Tone made lots of money, that's what,' says Woolly. 'They fed the pups so cheap you know but then they charged a lot of money when they sold them. They are bad people,' says he.

'We know that,' says I.

The first van roars into the field. People get out. Kind people, I can see. They step over to the pups and carefully start to wake them. A camera-man comes running up.

When he sees the pile of pups all dozing he laughs. 'What a picture!' says he. 'Lots of good people want these pups – the phones are hot already. But wait till they see this picture. What a winner it will be.' He lifts his camera and films while the sleepy pups open their eyes and yawn.

'The television people took pictures of me too,' says Woolly. He goes almost pink under his tight wool. 'Perhaps I am a star, Ratty? Like Chee? Do you think so?'

Of course he is a star, I think to myself. We are all stars in our way and perhaps he most of all.

But I do not want to be a star in a strange field with evening coming on. I want my friends about me and my own warm bed. White Horse feels the same.

'Do you know, Ratty,' says she, 'I believe I will trot back now to Farmer's field. Perhaps he will bring me some hay, or a slice of apple. He sometimes does. I would like that. I will go home.'

'White Horse, you are right,' says I. 'It is home time. Even those pups will have homes soon you know.'

'Look there!' bleats Woolly. 'I know who that is!'

So do we all. It is Hat Man. Come to find us. He runs up the field. His face is pale but he is smiling. He flings his arms around Cow's neck, then Woolly's. He touches my head with his finger. 'Dear friends,' says he, 'I have been a worried man but I knew you would be together. Please come home now and let us be comfortable.'

'You are right,' says Cow. 'The country is a tiring sort of place, you know, if you are used to the quiet city like me.'

'We should say goodbye to Horse,' says Woolly.

'Too late,' says I. I can see Horse's high back as she trots off down the road. 'It is home time and no mistake. Come, Woolly my friend. Let me climb up onto your curly back. Hat Man can take us home. We will see all our friends again and sleep in our own place.'

So that is what we do.

CHAPTER 11

It is morning time. I have slept in my own straw. My belly is full of fresh grain and a slice of apple. I am amongst my friends and in my own place. I am as happy as a ratty can be.

Woolly is telling his sheep friends all about his adventure. They are proud to be sheep and trot about their paddock like heroes.

I am sitting on a fence post talking to Cow. 'I wonder where Nip is now?' says I. 'Wherever those bad men go, they have taken a good doggo with them.'

'Doggos,' says Cow. 'You never know about a doggo.' Cow has had lots to do with doggos in her life and she has her own thoughts.

Here comes Hat Man, strolling up the path towards us. 'Look at what I have here!' says Hat Man. 'Look, Cow. This is the idea we talked of. Look at these!'

Hanging from his arm are two broad golden ribbons. 'One of these is for you, Cow,' says he. He carefully puts it over her big horns and onto her neck.

'Oh Cow!' says I. 'It is a beautiful ribbon but what is it for? And Cow, dear Cow, why are you wearing it round your neck?'

Cow smiles from one big cow ear to the other. 'Oh Ratty,' says she, 'it is Hat Man's idea. And what a good idea it is!'

'You see, Ratty,' says Hat Man smiling, 'I was so sad when Cow and Woolly ran off. I thought they must be unhappy here. Then I thought perhaps they just do not want to be shut in, you know. It is not good to be shut in.'

'So he got us these,' says Cow.

'But what are they?' I squeak. 'I do not understand!'

'See, Ratty,' says Cow, 'there is writing on the ribbon. I cannot read it but Hat Man has told me what it says. It says Ambassador Cow. That is what.'

'Ambassador?' says I. 'That is a big word. What does it mean?'

'It means I can go out into the city. And Woolly too. We will tell people about animals and the farm,' says Cow. 'We will go to schools, and shows, and all the places people go. We will be animal Ambassadors.'

'You will meet all sorts of people,' says Hat Man, 'and animals too. I will take this ribbon to Woolly now.' And off he goes.

'Today the mayor is coming to see us,' says Cow. 'He has a gold chain. That is what Hat Man says. There will be lots of cameras.'

'Look at me! Look at me!' bleats Woolly from his paddock. He has got his golden ribbon around his neck. He is dancing and whisking his tail. 'I am a hero. And now I am an Ambassador! I am the best lambkin ever!' says he.

Hat Man comes back to Cow. 'The cameras will be here soon, Cow,' says he. 'Then the Mayor has ideas for your first trip out. I do not suppose you want to come too, Ratty?' says he.

'No indeed,' says I. 'Ratties are not camera sort of folk. But ratties have adventures, you must agree.'

Hat Man smiles and nods. Then he looks across to

the high railway bank. 'You know,' says he, 'I could swear I saw a fox just now. Up on the railway bank. That would be a good place for a fox. Lots of food, and safe too. There are city foxes I know,' says he, 'but we have never had one at the farm. Our own fox. Now that would be something!'

He strolls off, humming to himself. Cow looks at me. I look back at her. She smiles. 'A city fox?' says she. 'Or a country fox that wants a rest and a quiet place and good friends? What do you think, Ratty?'

'We will see tomorrow,' says I, 'but I know what I think.'

And I smile my wide and whiskery rat smile.

THE ROAD TO THE RIVER

I love adventure. Ratties do.

So Ratty's thrilled when he gets the call to leave the peace and quiet of home. Urged on by Cow and Woolly, he sets off to rescue a friend who's in trouble. He heads for town and takes up with a brave little chihuahua who loves adventure as much as he does.

Then the nightmare begins.

The follow-up to *The Road to Somewhere* is a roller-coaster tale of fear and friendship, courage and conflict, told in Ratty's own special and charming words.

'A brilliantly told, gripping tale, with enduring and appealing characters, that explores difficult topics, as well as celebrating friendship.' *Junior*

'A page-turning thriller for younger readers, with captivating illustrations by Steve Dell.' *Junior Education*